COLE GOT CUCKED HARD

JACK HORNWOOD

Cole Got Cucked Hard
Jack Hornwood

3rd Edition
Copyright © 2020 Jack Hornwood
ISBN: 978-0-473-64706-3
Written in Aotearoa

www.jackhornwood.com

CHAPTER 1
COLE

I finish my coffee and set the cup down on the saucer. Across the table, Kenneth's cup is still full. It must be starting to get cold by now.

I glance around the room. The cafe has emptied out since about an hour ago when we got here. There's just a group chattering quietly a couple of tables away, and a lady reading the newspaper in the sun by the window.

I wonder to myself where the waiter has got to. I thought he would have been back to give me the bill by now. I consider going up to the counter to pay for breakfast, but it looks like they're a bit light on staff anyway; there's only one girl behind the counter, looking like she is unsuccessfully trying to do the maths required to split a bill for the group of seven that just finished up their breakfast.

I go back to reading my newspaper. I've already read all the articles that looked interesting, but now that I've some more time to fill, I start to flick back through the pages to see if any of the others that I'd ignored on my first pass could be worth a read.

Another minute or so ticks by. I wonder what's taking

Kenneth so long in the restroom. I hope he isn't sick or something. I figure I might as well drink his coffee though; another minute and it will be too cold to bother. No point wasting it. I reach over, pick it up, and knock it back in a few big gulps. It tastes better than mine, because I've been ordering them without sugar lately as part of a half-hearted attempt at losing weight.

It doesn't take long to discover that there's nothing else worth reading in the newspaper. I look around; our waiter from before is back behind the counter so I give him the head tilt and raised eyebrow to signal that he should bring the bill over. He nods and lifts a finger to indicate he'll be there in a moment.

I let my gaze linger for an extra couple of seconds. The guy is really sexy. Early twenties maybe, with that wispy, patchy kind of stubble that young guys get the first couple of times they grow it out. I can tell from his skinny jeans and the way the low cut of his t-shirt exposes his clavicle and the top of his chest that he must have a great body. Lean, like a swimmer or something.

I figure there's no harm in looking, just a little bit.

A few seconds later I hear footsteps behind me, and Kenneth lays his hand gently on my shoulder as he walks past me and sits down at the table.

"I drank your coffee," I tell him. "It was getting cold."

"That's okay," he replies.

"Are you okay? I was beginning to worry about you."

"Yeah. Sorry I took so long. I was feeling really rough, kept thinking I was gonna hurl. Maybe something I ate?"

"Or something you drank?" I ask, letting a hint of light-hearted accusation creep into my voice. "It was pretty late you stumbled in last night."

"I barely even drank!" He gives me his faux-wounded look. "I never get any sympathy from you!"

I have to laugh; it's totally true. "Okay. Sorry. I'll take you home, help you to bed, and tend to your needs all day."

He grins, that roguish, mischievous grin he always does. "All my needs?" I love how horny he always is.

I turn to signal the waiter again for the bill but he's already on his way over. As he hands over the bill he asks, "How was everything?" in a tone that indicates he's not really interested in how I found it at all.

I put my card down without really looking at the bill. "It was really good, thanks."

"And you, sir?" the waiter asks Kenneth. "Was everything to your liking?" That last sentence he says in a tone that's obviously flirtatious, and he flashes a smirk as he says it.

I'm right here, dickhead, I want to say. It really annoys me when guys try to flirt with Kenneth. Wherever we go, guys are always trying it on with him. And every time, they pretty much act like I'm not even there. I can understand why though, and it's not like I can really blame them. Kenneth is pure perfection. That boyish, youthful charm; he looks like he's twenty-one even though he's almost thirty. That captivating, mischievous smile, his piercing blue eyes, and silky smooth, golden skin. His body is incredible; slim and toned, with a bubble butt that's begging to be grabbed. I can see why all the guys are always after him, but it annoys me that none of them ever seem to appreciate the fact that he's obviously spoken for.

"Everything was great," Kenneth replies to the waiter, shooting back a similarly cheeky smile, the kind that makes me fucking furious. As the boy walks off with my credit card I shoot Kenneth an annoyed look. I don't know if he notices — and if he does, I'm not sure if he knows why I am annoyed. He doesn't seem to react at all.

The waiter comes back a minute later with my card and the receipt. As we stand up and head for the door he cheerily calls out "Hope to see you again soon." I'm pretty sure that isn't meant for both of us. I console myself with the fact that as hot as this guy might be, and as much as he might want to get it on with my man, I'm the one who gets to take Kenneth home.

CHAPTER 2
KENNETH

"Are you sure you're feeling up to it?" Cole asks as he parallel parks on the street outside Adam and Paul's place.

"I'm sure," I assure him. "I feel fine now, I swear."

It's nice of Cole to worry about me. This morning I'd told him that I wasn't feeling all that well, and ever since he's been worried that I'm not up to coming along to this party tonight. Truth be told, I'm feeling fine. I'd only told him I wasn't well because he'd been wondering why I took so long in the restroom at the cafe. It's not like I could tell him the real reason, which was that I'd been getting my ass nailed in the toilet cubicle by the waiter.

The guy had given me the eye pretty much as soon as we'd sat down at our table, and I'd seen him checking me out the whole time we'd been sitting there eating our breakfast. I'd shot glances back at him whenever Cole wasn't paying attention, and by the time I'd finished my bacon and eggs we both knew where things were headed. So when I was sitting there about to have my second coffee of the day, and I saw him headed towards the toilets, I was in there after him like a flash.

I'd found him standing at the urinal taking a piss, and he'd turned his head to watch as I walked past him to one of the stalls. I didn't close the door behind me; I just dropped my jeans and my underwear, and braced myself against the wall with my hands. It had only taken a few seconds before he was in there behind me, running his hands over my ass and reaching round to fondle my nuts and my already semi-hard shaft. It was only few more seconds before he spat into his hand, pulled my cheeks apart and started loosening up my hole with his fingers, then a few more seconds before his cock head was pushing against my waiting hole and slowly working its way in.

I'd expected it to be a quick fuck; a lot of guys seem to cum faster when it's a seedy public fuck like that; I think it's the added thrill of the chance of being caught. Not to mention most guys cum faster when it's raw. But this guy seemed to go for a decent amount of time. He started slow, and his long, slender dick made me whimper each time he pushed it right to the hilt. Once or twice he took it right out, then shoved it all the way back in with a single, forceful stroke that made me cry out. "Shut up," he'd whispered, chuckling to himself and giving me a slap on the ass. "You don't want your boyfriend to hear, do you?" But that just made me hornier.

After getting progressively faster, he'd started really pumping my ass. He pulled my head back by my hair so my back was arched, and he nibbled on my earlobe as he rammed his dick in and out, getting faster and more urgent. Then as he let out a grunt that was barely audible, I felt him blow his load. I could feel his cock twitch inside me two or three times as my ass filled up with his warm seed, and his whole body convulsed. Then he was out of me, and a few seconds later he was out the door.

I'd pulled up my pants, washed up and headed back to our table. Cole had already drunk my coffee, and was wondering what had taken so long. That guy must have been fucking me for at least twenty minutes or so, if not longer. So

I'd made up the line about feeling unwell; it was the only excuse I could think of on the spot.

I'm starting to regret it now. Partly because despite all the subtle hints I dropped all day, he still hasn't fucked me, which means I still haven't had the chance to cum yet. But also because now, more than eight hours later Cole just can't leave it alone.

"If you start to feel sick, just let me know," he tells me as we both get out of the car. "We can go home any time." I'm starting to think that maybe Cole is actually just looking for an excuse not to have to do this party; he's never been much of a partier the whole time we've been together. But there's no chance we're leaving any time soon; I'm still horny as hell, and I know I'm going to get some dick here tonight.

Paul greets us at the door and welcomes us in. We do the obligatory birthday well-wishes and small-talk as he grabs our coats and hangs them up by the door. As Cole makes his way to the kitchen to grab us a couple of drinks, Paul leans in close and says, "Adam tells me you're my birthday present tonight."

"You know you don't have to wait till your birthday to have me," I whisper back.

He laughs. "Yeah I know. Listen, when I give you the nod, head up to my room. Adam will keep Cole busy. Once I'm done we'll swap. Cool?"

"Definitely."

At that moment Cole reappears with a couple of beers. As he hands me one I tell him, "Hey, I'll take it easy and be sober driver tonight if you want to have a few."

We wander into the living room. There's already a few of the regular gang, and a couple of friends of friends, in amongst Paul's work colleagues and other strangers. We chill out for a bit, knock back a couple of beers, and catch up with the crew. Adam, Paul's husband, keeps Cole well supplied with drinks, enough that he starts to get pretty lively after an hour or so.

Other than our usual crew — most of whom have already fucked me before — there aren't many hot guys at the party. The bulk of the people are from Paul's work, so they're either women or straight couples. There's one silver fox who I flirt madly with for a few minutes, who's obviously into me but either too cautious or too respectful to suggest anything. And there's a couple of hot younger guys who I keep giving the eye to from across the room, who I go introduce myself to. They're definitely down for something, and my reputation has obviously preceded me because they seem to already know that I'll fuck anything with a cock. So we swap numbers and promise to meet up for a threesome some time soon. Although they're hot, they're a little dull though, and after a while I'm starting to get impatient.

Finally after what seems like almost forever, Paul walks past. He gives me a subtle nod as he starts heading up the stairs. I quickly excuse myself from the conversation I'm having, and follow him. Before I go up the stairs I pause to make sure Cole isn't around to see. But he's nowhere to be found; either being distracted by Adam or chatting to one of the gang out in the kitchen or the garden.

I run up the stairs as fast as I'm able to go without attracting attention. The door to Adam and Paul's room at the end of the hall is open, and Paul is standing in the doorway expectantly. "Get in here, bitch," he growls playfully, moving aside for me to step through the doorway and grabbing my ass as I do.

Before he's even shut the door I'm unbuttoning my shirt. He starts unbuttoning his too, and as he does he kisses me roughly, his tongue slipping its way into my mouth. As I pull my shirt off he runs his hands up and down my chest, his lips and tongue still locked with mine. I fumble with his belt and his fly, desperate to get at that cock. Shirtless now, he pushes against me slowly, forcing me to step backwards till I feel the bed against the back of my legs. I let myself fall back onto the bed, and Paul is immediately on top of me, the hair on his chest tickling my chest as he writhes back and forward on top of me.

Paul releases his lock on my lips, and kisses my neck. It drives me fucking wild when he does that, and I can't help but let out a half whimper, half moan of delight. With his tongue he traces down my neck, my collarbone, my chest, and gently licks my left nipple for a few seconds. Then he continues to trace a path down my abs, my belly button, to where the trail of hair starts between my hips. He unbuttons my jeans and runs his hand over the outline of my rock-hard dick, which is straining to get loose from my underwear.

At that point he stands up. He grabs my jeans by the ankles and tugs hard. My jeans are tight and it takes him a few firm tugs to get them off me. Once he has though, he grabs me by the hips and flips me over, face down on the bed. Slowly he peels off my trunks, and slides a finger slowly but firmly across my hole. He spreads my ass-cheeks apart and dives in there with his face, kissing and licking my ass. His short beard tickles the skin around my hole, but nowhere near as much as his tongue tickles my hole itself as he flicks it around at speed.

"Fuck yes," I sigh as he licks my hole. I've missed Paul's rim jobs. I push myself up onto my knees so he can get in deeper, and I feel his big tongue push its way into my opening. "Fuck yes!" I gasp.

After a minute or so he stops. A second later I feel the cold shock of lube being applied to my asshole. With two fingers he pushes it in and gently massages it around. Then a second later his fingers are replaced by his cock firmly pressing against my waiting hole.

He pushes it into me slowly, holding on to my hips. I gasp with the feeling of his big, thick dick invading my hole and pushing further and further in. He leans over so his chest is pressed against my back, and he nuzzles the back of my neck. "Fuck, I love your tight little cunt," he whispers in my ear. He pulls his cock half way out, and then slowly drives it all the way back in to the base.

"Fuck. Oh my god." I'm in fucking ecstasy. "Fuck me," I beg.

"You want to be fucked?" he replies. "I'll fuck you alright." With that he pulls out, holds the tip of his cock at the mouth of my hole for a second, then with one huge, forceful stroke he rams that dick inside me.

I let out a moan that's almost a scream.

"Ssshhhh," he whispers. But then he pulls out and rams it back in just as hard, and it makes me wail again with the combination of pain and intense bliss.

With that he turns into a fucking animal. He starts to pound my ass with force. He grips my hips, and stands up behind me to get maximum leverage. His big, thick cock rams my hole over and over again. With every hard thrust my whimpers and my moans get louder, till he puts a hand over my mouth to muffle the noise. "Quiet bitch, or do you want the whole party to hear?"

At that point I really couldn't give a fuck whether every person in the house can hear me moan and wail. I'm loving this fuck so much I've almost forgotten where I am; and anyway, the thought of fifty guests downstairs hearing me get my ass wrecked makes me even more turned on.

"Fuck," I pant, although the hand over my mouth muffles my words beyond recognition. "I love your dick. Fuck me, fuck me." Not that I need to ask. He doesn't stop pounding my ass for a second. He just gets harder and harder, and faster and faster. As he pounds away at my hole he growls, and grunts, and whispers dirty shit in my ear. His breath on my ear and neck sends shivers down me, at the same time as the pounding sends convulsions through my whole body. He pushes me down onto the bed and pins me down with his body, pounding my ass into the mattress. Then, he lets out a growl like a tiger, and his whole body twitches as he blows his load inside of me. I can feel his cock pulse three, four, five times as he coats my guts in his seed. Then his thrusts slow right down, and he collapses on top of me in a panting heap.

"Fuck that was amazing," he says breathlessly. "I love fucking that beautiful little cunt of yours." I can feel his chest heaving against my back as he lays there panting on top of me, and I can feel his cock start to soften inside my ass. After a minute or so he slowly pulls out, and I feel a trickle of his cum escape as he does. I clench my ass; I don't want to lose another drop.

Paul gives me a quick peck on the cheek and gets up off me. I turn and look up to see him buttoning up his shirt and the fly of his pants, neither of which he'd bothered to take off properly before fucking me. "You stay there," he told me. "Adam won't be far off. He's real keen to fuck you tonight, boy."

Paul slowly opens the bedroom door and peers out to make sure the coast is clear. Then he's gone, shutting the door quietly behind him.

I stay where I am, face down on the bed. I'm glad to have a minute to get myself together; I'm still feeling breathless from the fucking I've just been given. My respite doesn't last long though, as it must be less than a minute later when I hear footsteps in the hallway outside. I don't look up as the door opens, then slowly closes again.

"Fuck that's an amazing ass," Adam says with what almost sounds like awe in his voice. He places his hand gently on it and rubs gently, his hand slowly making its way towards my sloppy hole. He runs his finger over my fuckhole, then pushes it a centimetre or so in. "All lubed up for me."

A second later and his tongue is up against my hole, licking ever so gently. "It tastes like Paul," he says approvingly. Then he starts lapping at it like he's trying to eat an ice cream before it melted. "Fuck," he pauses to say. "You've got the most amazing cunt." It feels incredible, his tongue flittering over my hole, then working its way in.

"Fuck me," I beg. "Please fuck me."

He happily obliges. In a second his tongue is gone, replaced with his cockhead pressing up against my ass. "Hope you're ready, boy," he says. And with a forceful push, he drives his dick balls-deep inside me.

"Fuck!" I cry out, mostly with pain. I grab a pillow and bury my face in it, just in time for him to quickly pull out and then drive his dick back inside me in a massive push. I scream into the pillow, hoping it'll muffle my cries enough that the guests downstairs wouldn't hear.

Adam leans down until I can feel his breath on my neck. "You like that, bitch?" he whispers to me.

It's so god damn painful, but at the same time my ass feels like it's complete, impaled on the end of Adam's thick cock. "I love it," I whisper back.

"Good boy." With that he starts to pump his dick in and out of me ferociously, gripping my hips to provide extra force each time he slams into me. I'm in cockwhore heaven; I can feel his ballsack slap against mine each time he slams my sloppy ass, and I start to moan and mewl like a little bitch each time he drives himself into me.

The sound of the door opening behind me instantly brings me back into reality though. Panicked, I turn around, expecting to see Cole there. It's the moment I've dreaded - and fantasised about - for months.

But it's not Cole. It's James, standing there in the door way with a giant shit-eating grin on his face. "Thought I'd find you two in here," he says as he closes the door behind him. "Don't stop on my account."

Fuck, that's a relief. Even though the thought of Cole catching me gets me insanely horny, I definitely am not ready to have that conversation with him yet. Especially not tonight, at a party with a bunch of his friends — most of whom have fucked me at one time or another.

Adam carries on pounding my ass enthusiastically, as James unzips his fly to reveal a long, lean uncut cock. He shoves it in my face, and I open up my mouth to let him slide it inside.

The two of them fuck me from both ends. Adam keeps getting harder and faster, and James grabs me by the back of the jaw and face-fucks me with equal force. He keeps pushing his dick right down my throat as far as it can go, and I flail and gag each time it cuts off my air passage. "Suck that dick," he orders as he pulls it out and shoves it back in again.

"Fuck," Adam growls. "I'm gonna cum." His thrusts get suddenly faster, and the whole bed is shaking with the force of him pounding my ass. "Fuck…. Oh fuck. Get ready bitch, get ready for my load." And with that I feel his cock drive into me even harder than before, and begin to pulse as he fills my ass with his load. "Fuck," he moans, as his cock pulses and pulses.

That is enough to set James off. I feel his dick pulse once, and I feel a wad of cum on my tongue. As he starts cumming James pulls his dick out of my mouth, so that the second and third spurt shoot all over my face. The cum keeps dripping out, and I greedily lick it up as fast as it emerges.

Adam slaps me on the ass. "Good boy," he says breathlessly. He scoops up a bit of the cum that's leaking out of my ass, and uses it to lube up my cock. He starts jacking me off at a leisurely pace as he sits down to catch his breath. After the fucking I've just had, it only takes me thirty seconds or so of him jacking me off before I blow a massive load all over the bed.

"What a cumwhore," James mocks me. "I love it when Cole brings you along to parties."

I wonder whether Cole's heard any of what just happened.

We've probably been pretty loud, especially towards the end with the moaning and with the thumping of the bed against the wall. I figure I should probably get back to him before he comes to look for me. Though I should probably clean James' cum off my face before I head downstairs to rejoin the party. First, though, I need to lie here a couple of minutes longer and catch my breath. I am fucking wrecked.

CHAPTER 3
COLE

I have no idea how I managed to get this drunk. I don't remember drinking that much tonight. On second thoughts, maybe it has been a few. Adam just seems to keep handing them to me — cocktails, beers, sparkling wine — and now that I think about it, I feel like I probably haven't been without a drink the whole time I've been here. And those cocktails before were strong too, I think. I remember thinking that a couple of times. I think. It's kind of hard to remember now.

It's not like I'm paralytic or anything. I'm just a little hazy, my words sound a little slurred. And I keep losing my train of thought. And my balance, I keep losing my balance.

It's definitely not intentional. I don't even drink that much anymore. Back in the day I used to party fairly hard. But since I hit thirty I've slowed it down substantially: a couple of glasses of wine over dinner is pretty much as rowdy as I get.

It's not like it's that kind of party, either. It's all pretty civilised. Lots of guys from Paul's work. Lots of civilised people making civilised small talk. I catch myself swaying a little bit and hope I'm not making a fool of myself.

Adam's been talking to me for the last couple of minutes, but somewhere along the way I must have tuned out. He's standing at the kitchen bench making cocktails, so I offer to help him cut limes and mint. Maybe working with sharp knives isn't the brightest idea right now, but I think having something to concentrate on will help.

"Get Paul something good for his birthday?" I ask.

"Sure did," Adam replies with a sly grin. "I organised something special for him."

I can tell from the way he replies that it must be something dirty. "What is it?"

He just laughs dismissively. "It's a secret," he replies. "I know he's gonna like it though. And it's something we can both use."

I know I'm not going to get any more out of him; he's pretty cagey when he wants to be.

I feel a hand rest on my shoulder as James' voice behind me asks, "Where's your boyfriend tonight?" He tries to make the question sound casual, but I recognise that tone in his voice. He's always asking about Kenneth, and always fawning over him whenever he's around. I bet if he had half a chance he'd try it on with him.

"He's here. Somewhere. Must be out in the living room entertaining the accountants."

"I bet he'd be good entertainment." There's that tone again.

"Give it a rest man!" I'm trying to make it sound jokey, but to be honest I'm pretty annoyed at the way James is always either trying to creep onto Kenneth, or just insinuating a bunch of stuff about him. James can be a real dick sometimes; it's part of the reason we don't hang out that much any more. But I'm pretty used to it, and it's not worth getting into a whole thing about.

Paul comes in, grabs Adam from behind, and plants a kiss on his neck. He whispers something in his ear, and Adam turns around and kisses him. "Can you take over from me with these mojitos?" he asks.

"Sure." He grabs soda from the fridge as Adam wanders off into the living room. He starts to mix the drinks, and I see him glance down at where I'm fumbling with the knife trying to cut mint. "Hey bud, how you doing there?"

"I'm pretty good," I reply. "I drank more than I meant to."

Paul laughs. "That's what parties are for. How about you leave the knife-work to me."

I think that's a good idea. I set the knife down. "Maybe I should go see how Kenneth is doing. Rescue him from the accountants."

"He's fine. He can take care of himself. Besides, the accountants are actually not bad, if you can believe it. Grab yourself another drink, dude. You're already half-cut so you might as well make a night of it. Maybe we'll have you dancing on the table-tops by the end of the night."

A couple of people walk in and start talking to Paul about something. I lose track pretty quick. I look around for James but he's disappeared, so I wander back out into the living room. No sign of Kenneth; I wonder where he's got to. Maybe the shop talk with Paul's workmates got too much for him. Or maybe he's outside smoking. He does that occasionally when he's drinking. I do a one-eighty and head to the back yard, where I find a few people milling around chatting in the warm night air, but no sign of Kenneth.

I turn to head back inside, and Paul's there in front of me. He pats me on the back and hands me a mojito. "Hang out with me out here, Cole," he says, "while I have a sly cigarette." He sits down on the steps and I sit down next to him. It feels so good to sit down. I could almost lie down on and go to sleep right here on the concrete pavers.

Paul is rambling away, I've kind of lost track what he's talking about.

The music sounds louder all of a sudden as the door to the

house opens. A couple of guys I haven't met before are laughing hysterically.

Paul greets them: "Ray, Dougie! Come grab a seat. What's going on?"

"Man, someone is fucking upstairs, bro!" I don't know if the one talking is Ray or Dougie. "Sounds like someone's really getting it."

"Didn't know it was that kind of party," the other one laughs. "Maybe I should go join in."

"Whoever that lucky bottom is, he's wailing so loud you can hear it over the music!"

They suddenly go quiet, and stop laughing. Is it just me, or do things seem to have turned awkward all of a sudden? Oh shit, maybe it's Adam up there. I look at Paul's face but it doesn't give anything away.

"I like my guests to have fun, you know," Paul chuckles. "Glad whoever's up there is having a good time. Talking of fucking at parties, how was that trip to Fire Island?" Even for someone as half-wasted as me, that clumsy attempt to change the subject is pretty obvious. I wonder what's going on up there. I wonder if it is Adam fucking.

Ray and Dougie start talking all about their sex holiday. I try follow the conversation but before long I've lost track again. I sit there trying to listen for a few minutes but I'm starting to get bored. Plus I feel like if I don't move soon I might actually fall asleep here. I struggle to my feet, wobbling a little bit. "I'm going to go inside."

I walk back into the house. I look back and see the guys laughing. Is one of them shooting looks at me? Are they laughing at me? Or am I just paranoid? I'm probably just paranoid. To be honest, it's really hard following what's going on by this stage.

I circulate through the living room, but still no sign of Kenneth. I turn and head into the kitchen, and grab myself a glass of water from the tap.

A pair of arms wrap around me from behind. I crane my head to find that it's Kenneth. He kisses me on the neck. "Hey babe. How you going?"

"Where have you been?" I ask. "I was looking round for you."

"I was just out in the living room." He looks confused. He sizes me up. "By the looks of it, maybe you couldn't find me because you can't see straight."

I try protest for a second, but then I realise that I am actually pretty far gone.

"Maybe we should get you home," he suggests. I nod at that, and rest my tired head on his shoulder for a second.

"We're gonna get out of here," Kenneth says. I look up, and find Adam standing there. "I think this one's about ready to pass out."

Adam looks at me sympathetically. "Glad you had a good night, bud. Thanks for coming tonight." He gives me a pat on the back. "Now get outta here, before you vomit on my kitchen floor!"

Kenneth looks at me with an apologetic expression. "Hey babe I'm really sorry. I know I said I'd drive, but I actually had a bit to drink. So I think we'd better get a cab. It's all good though — hand on heart I promise I'll come pick up the car tomorrow."

Adam laughs at that, though I'm not sure why. Maybe it's because it's so predictable. I'm sure he does this every time. I tell him it's all good. Kenneth gets his phone out and orders a car.

I'm giving Adam a hug when Paul comes in. "Good timing," Adam tells him. "These guys are just leaving."

I give Paul a drunken hug. "Happy birthday, man."

As we're headed out the door Kenneth says, "See you tomorrow," and that gets another laugh from Adam; again, I'm not sure what I'm missing there. But I'm probably just too drunk to get the joke.

Outside, waiting for the uber, Kenneth asks me, "Did you have a good time tonight babe?"

"Yeah." I rest my head on his shoulder again. I'm so sleepy right now. "You?"

"Had a blast."

CHAPTER 4
KENNETH

It's a stunner outside. Blue sky, a slight breeze, and barely a cloud in sight. It would be a crime to let an afternoon like this go by without getting out in the sunshine. More to the point, it's a perfect afternoon to flaunt my body and see if I can attract a few guys to dick me down in the sunshine.

"Out for a run," I call out to Cole as I pull my running shoes on.

"Okay babe, have fun!"

I wonder for a second if Cole ever gets suspicious when I go out running. Especially the times I go out wearing next to nothing, and come home smelling of cum and other guys' sweat. If he ever does notice he never says a thing though.

I close the front door behind me, stretch a little on the verandah, and then I'm off out the gate. As I jog down the street I can feel my cock and balls bouncing up and down. I love the feeling of freeballing in my running shorts; hopefully when the guys look — and they'll definitely be looking, no doubt about it — they'll notice my package bouncing around in my little mesh shorts as I run.

My usual route takes me to the end of our street and onto the main road. About two hundred metres down that road is a block of shops, including a cafe with tables that spill out onto the wide footpath. As I jog past I notice a couple of guys sitting out the front, and grin to myself as I see both of them eyeing me up. I glance back as I pass them, and one of them quickly shifts his gaze to pretend he wasn't looking. The other one keeps looking; he either doesn't care whether I notice, or he wants to make sure I notice.

Another three hundred metres or so down that road, I pass the house of a guy who'd fucked me a few times when I'd been out on my run. But it looks like there's no one home today, and he hadn't been on any of the apps when I'd checked not long before I left home, so I guess I'm out of luck there.

Another hundred metres or so and I'm passed by a guy on his bike. He turns to check me out as he passes, and he's so distracted he almost rides straight into a parked car. He realises just in time, swerves, and carries on. I fucking love the effect I have on guys when they see me out running, wearing nothing but these tiny shorts and my running shoes.

There are a few cars parked around the entrance to the park when I get there. That's a promising sign. I jog past a few families chilling out at the playground, and take the path that leads into the trees. It's uphill a bit from here, so this is where I usually start to get a bit of a sweat on when it's a hot day. That's always good; I know it drives the guys crazy when they see the sweat beading on my chest and my back.

It's about a five minute uphill run to the best cruising spot. When I get to the big grass picnic area though, it's empty. I stop and sit down at the picnic table to catch my breath and see what talent turns up. It's nice up here; there's this big old tree overhanging the table, letting through dappled sunlight but casting just enough of a shadow to provide a bit of refuge from the hot afternoon sun. There's the lightest of breezes, and I love the way it tickles my bare skin just a little.

It's not long before I've got company. A young guy, maybe

in his early twenties, wanders up the path. Blonde hair sticking out from beneath his baseball cap, tanned skin with the lightest shade of fuzz on his arms. I can tell by the way his t-shirt hangs off his upper body that he's decently built. He gives me a look that lingers a couple of seconds too long to be innocent, but he doesn't say anything, just walks past. When he gets to the end of the clearing where the path starts again, he looks back at me, but he doesn't make any kind of signal. Guess he's kinda shy, which is always a turn-on.

I give him a few seconds, then I get up and jog up the path in the same direction. As I pass him I look back at him, letting my gaze fix long enough to make it pretty obvious what I want. Then a few metres up I turn off the path and and slow to a walk. I know this spot. If you push past the foliage of this big bush there's a narrow almost-path that takes you to another tiny clearing that's not visible from the track. I push through the branches, and as I do I look back to make sure he can see where I'm headed.

As I start down the path I hear him pushing through the branches behind me. This time I don't look back though. I keep walking till I reach the spot. When I emerge into the little clearing I turn around and wait for the guy to catch up.

He emerges from the trees and stops. Looks me up and down. Gives me a nod. "Hey." He seems awkward. Like maybe he doesn't do this very often.

"Hey." I take a couple of steps towards him. Into his personal space.

The guy hesitates for a few seconds, just stands there looking at me. So I gently lay a hand on his torso, and step even closer, so now my face is inches from his. I gently kiss his neck, as I run my hand up his chest. That gets him started; he kisses me on the lips, first softly, then more forcefully. He puts his hands on my lower back, and runs them down until they're cupping my ass cheeks in my little mesh shorts.

We make out for a minute or so. I run my hands up and

down his chest, exploring the shape of his body. He's lean, muscular. Strong chest and shoulders. I run a hand down to his shorts, feeling his cock through the fabric of his shorts. He's long, fairly thick, and definitely ready to go.

I drop down to my knees, and pull his shorts down just enough to reveal his underwear. His cock is straining through his briefs, the shape perfectly visible through the white fabric. I kiss it, through the fabric, up and down the shaft, before I slowly reach in and extract it from the confines of the fabric.

It's beautiful. I mean, they all are. There's something about men's cocks that just never ceases to mesmerise me. This one's no exception. I take the tip in my mouth, and massage it lightly with my tongue. He moans, and almost instantly I can taste the salty precum he's leaking.

"Fuck that's good, bro," he sighs. I take it a little deeper, still letting my tongue flitter across the head. He moans some more.

After a few minutes I take it out to catch my breath. "Can you lick my balls, bro?" he asks. "I love getting my balls licked."

I oblige. I run my tongue in long, slow motions across his ballsack and he gasps with pleasure. "Fuck yeah, just like that." He's really getting into it; I can feel his body start to relax as I lap away at those low-hangers. I bet he was nervous about this, about coming to this cruising spot, but now he's forgotten all about anything other than my mouth on his nuts.

I migrate back to his cock. I give the head another lick, then I take the whole thing in my mouth and start sucking him off properly. "Bro!" he moans. His cock is so salty; his cock is drooling so much precum. I love it when they leak like that. I take his cock deep, right down to the back of my throat, and massage it all the way to the tip with my tongue each time I bring it almost out of my mouth.

"Fuck!" All of a sudden he pulls my mouth off him. I look

up. "Sorry man, you're getting me so close I had to stop." He pauses. "Can I fuck you?"

"Sure." I get up off my knees, and turn around. I back up against him, so that his hard, wet cock is nestled up against my ass.

"You got any rubbers?" he asks.

"Nope. Don't worry about it. I'm on PrEP." I slowly pull down my shorts, and push back onto him so that the tip of his cock is right up against my hole. I already got his shaft so wet that I know it will slip in easily enough, even without lube. I slowly push against his cock, and I can feel it start to slide in just a little. The guy hesitates, so I push back a little bit harder. I feel it open me up as it slides in a few centimetres. Then he does the rest, pushing it the whole way in.

"Fuck that feels good!" He starts pumping, using one arm to pull me tight against him as he fucks me from behind. With the other he grabs my chin and turns my head as far back as it will go, so he can stick his tongue down my throat while he pounds my ass. Then, as his thrusts become harder, he shoves me by the shoulders so I bend over for him, and he jackhammers into my ass . "Fuck yeah," he grunts. "Fuck, your ass is good."

I know this guy's not going to last long. He really pounds me for another minute or so, then he warns me, "Dude, I'm gonna cum."

I love this bit.

With a grunt and one last thrust I feel him empty his balls inside of me. I hear him breathing hard as he recovers from blowing his load, then slowly he pulls out of me. I feel a trickle of cum run down my thigh.

He pulls up his pants. "Thanks, bro." And then like a flash, probably feeling hella awkward all of a sudden, he's disappeared back into the trees.

I'm still just standing there with my shorts around my

knees when I see the guy watching me from across the clearing. I wonder how long he's been there.

"Enjoy the show?"

"It was hot," he replies. He steps out into the sun of the clearing, and I get a good look at him. Jeans, t-shirt, cap. Stubble. Early forties, maybe. Decently in shape.

"You want a turn?" I ask.

"Of course." He crosses the clearing, and walks right up to me. Grabs my hard cock in one hand, and my ass in the other. His finger explores my cummy hole while he strokes me slowly. "Get on all fours," he orders.

I get down on the ground, on all fours. He takes off his shirt, his shoes, his jeans. Once he's naked he kneels down on the ground behind me, and starts to lick the last guy's cum from my hole. He gets his tongue in nice and deep, digging the cum out of my freshly fucked hole. It feels good: a warm, soft massage, after the jackhammer fuck I just got."Fuck that's tasty," he tells me as he laps up the cum.

Once he's got out all he can, he lines up his cock. "You ready for another one?"

"Of course." I'm always ready for more cock.

I feel his bare cock slide in slowly. It feels thick but it glides almost effortlessly in, my hole is so well stretched and lubed by this stage. He grunts. "Fuck that's a good hole." He pushes right in to the hilt, and lets out a deep breath of appreciation as he holds it there for a few seconds. Then he starts to pump me with slow, deep strokes.

The sun is warm on my back, and he pumps away at a leisurely pace in this warm patch of sunshine in this tiny clearing in the woods. It's nice; so often these daytime part hookups are so quick and furtive. I mean don't get me wrong, I love a seedy, illicit, quick fuck when you're both trying to finish before you get caught. But sometimes it's nice to take your time, and enjoy fucking in the outdoors under the afternoon sun.

The guy pulls out. He lies on the ground, and I get on top. I lower myself down onto him, and he fucks me lazily as I ride him. I bend down and make out with him. He's a good kisser; he holds my head by the base of my skull and pulls it in. I writhe up and down languidly, kissing him, feeling the beads of sweat start to form on my back as we fuck in the summer heat.

Although the pace is pleasant, my need to be dicked down hard begins to take over, and I start to ride him harder. I kiss him more intensely. "I want you to cum inside me," I whisper in his ear between kisses.

"Yeah?"

"Yeah. I want your load."

"Okay then, you got it." He grabs my hips and starts to fuck me hard. With me bucking up and down with all the force I can, and him thrusting his hips from below, he's getting in deep and hitting my prostate really hard. Each time it hits, it sends a wave of pleasure through my body.

I feel it building. "I'm gonna cum!"

That makes him fuck me even harder. I bear down on his cock as hard as I can, and grind against it as I feel my balls start to unload. My dick explodes with rope after rope of cum, that shoot up into the air and come splashing down on the stranger's chest. The second they hit his skin, it sets him off. He lets out a moan and I can feel him unload inside me.

I collapse on top of him, and we lie there like that for a minute or so. Our breathing is heavy and almost in time, but gradually mine returns to normal, and his starts to do the same.

He extracts his cock from me, and I dismount him and roll onto the grass. For a few minutes we just lie there in the sun and chat; I find out that his name's Warren, and he's a bit of a regular at this cruising spot. He tells me about how he started coming here back when he was married, because that was his only option; and how even though he's now out and single, and doesn't need to cruise parks anymore, he still loves it on days like this when the sun's shining. "And when little sluts like you are out in their running shorts," he laughs.

Eventually we get up. He starts to get dressed, and I put my shorts back on. I give him a kiss, tell him I hope to see him round again, and set off back home.

As I jog home I can feel the cum trickle out of my loose hole and down my leg. I love that feeling. I hope it's not making too noticeable a wet patch in the seat of my shorts though, as I jog down the busy road past the shops again.

When I get home Cole's in the garden. "How was your run?" he asks.

"Great!" I stop and give him a kiss as I catch my breath.

He puts a hand on my hip. "I love it when you're sweaty like this. And you look damn good in those shorts." He lowers his hand down to my ass.

"Oh really? Maybe you should come upstairs and show me how much you like it."

He looks excited at that idea. As we head upstairs I think to myself, I hope he doesn't notice the cum leaking down my legs. Or the dirty patches on my knees from when I was on all fours getting my ass pounded. Or on second thoughts, maybe I hope he does notice.

CHAPTER 5
COLE

I'm out in the front garden pulling weeds out from between the paving stones when Kenneth comes back from his run. I get up to greet him as he opens the gate. "How was your run?" I ask him.

"Great!"

He looks amazing. He's in these tiny little blue mesh running shorts that cling to his bubble butt and the bulge of his balls. He's shirtless, with beads of sweat on his forehead and neck, and the golden skin of his torso glistening with a sweaty sheen. "I love it when you're sweaty like this." I put my hands on him; I feel the warm, slick sweat on his lower back. And you look damn good in those shorts." I slide my hand down onto his tiny shorts and grasp his ass firmly.

"Oh really?" He gives me a mischievous look. "Maybe you should come upstairs and show me how much you like it."

I don't need any more convincing than that. I was already feeling mildly horny, so seeing Kenneth looking like that gets me going one hundred percent, instantly.

He takes my hand and leads me inside. We start up the stairs towards the bedroom. Standing behind him on the stairs I watch his tight ass in those tight shorts as he walks up each step. Goddamn it, that ass looks good. I tug on his hand to stop him, and standing on the step below him I pull him back into me so he can feel my dick starting to harden against this thigh.

I can't take any more waiting. I start to peel his shorts down. They're wet with sweat, and they cling to every contour. I slowly pull them down his legs, and he kicks them the rest of the way off.

I apply just a little bit of pressure to his back. "Get down," I tell him.

He gets down onto his knees, right there on the stairs. His knees on one stair, his head resting on his elbows a couple of stairs higher, his ass up in the air. I kneel on the next stair down, so my face is level with his ass.

"You've got the most beautiful ass in the world," I tell him, to which I get a chuckle in response.

I caress his bubble butt for a bit before I take a finger and gently rub it against his hole. It feels surprisingly slick. It even looks a little slick around the hole, like he's already lubed it up for me. I apply a little pressure, and my finger starts to slide in easily. Kenneth lets out the little whimper that he always seems to do the moment he's first penetrated. I only ease my finger in about a centimetre though, just to tease him. Then I withdraw and get down onto my knees behind him.

I gently lick the underside of Kenneth's testicles, and run my tongue along his taint. It's so salty with sweat. When I reach his hole I gently lap at it with my tongue. That salty taste of sweat is even stronger around his hole.

No, wait. That's not sweat.

I push my tongue in deeper, exploring the taste. It's salty, for sure, but it's definitely not sweat. I know cum when I taste it.

I gasp and pull my face out of Kenneth's ass. For a moment I kneel there on the stair, my head swimming. I'm imagining it, right? I must be. There's no way it could be cum. Surely.

Kenneth looks back at me. "You okay babe?"

I almost can't answer. I have no idea what to say. Does he actually have another guy's cum in his ass? Should I ask him? No, I can't. What if I'm wrong; he'd be so hurt by the accusation. But what if I'm right? As that thought crosses my mind, I feel my cock twitch, and I realise it's suddenly got twice as hard as it was a few seconds ago.

"Babe?"

I snap back into the moment. "I'm all good," I reply. I tentatively I lean in, and gently tease the rim of his hole with my tongue again. The taste is not as strong now. In fact it's so faint that I figure I must have been imagining it. I have to know though. I take my middle finger and massage his hole with it, then slowly slide it inside him. I add my index finger, so I've got two fingers inside. He moans as I push them in as far as I can go, then I pull them out.

I look at my fingers. They're slick and wet. I hold them up to my nose and, sure enough, they smell of cum. Just to be absolutely sure, I put them in my mouth and taste them. The taste is unmistakeable.

The bastard. How the fuck could he do this to me? This hurts, like actual, physical pain. I feel like someone's kicked me in the stomach. In this moment I feel so many emotions hit me at once that I can barely register what they all are. Humiliation. Anger. Grief. I can feel the fury and the jealousy start to rise out of my stomach, and I can hear my heartbeat thumping in my head. But at the same time I can feel my cock straining against my pants, harder and more swollen than it's been in as long as I can remember. As awful as I feel right now, I'm suddenly the horniest I've been in months.

I enthusiastically plunge my tongue back into Kenneth's ass, driving it as deep as I can to try and lap out every bit of seed I can reach. I grab him by the hips and hold on so I can get in even deeper. I'm like an aardvark in an ant's nest, driving my tongue in and out of his sloppy, wet hole to get the prize hiding inside.

Kenneth seems to appreciate it. His moans get louder and his little whimpers become more plaintive and breathless the more I eat his ass out. His noises, along with the taste of the cum, are driving me so wild I can barely hold it in anymore. I furiously unbutton my pants and pull out my cock, and in a single thrust I drive it into Kenneth's ass. He cries out, and in that second I empty a massive load of cum inside him. I spurt hard, seven or eight times, each time letting out a groan of absolute relief. It's like every bit of rage and sadness and hurt erupts out of me in ropes of cum, coating the walls of Kenneth's ass.

I collapse on top of him, my chest heaving.

After I catch my breath I reach for Kenneth's cock, which is still hard. I wrap my hand around it and start to jerk him off, but he gently brushes my hand away. "I'm okay," he says, craning his neck back and kissing me. "Thank you. That was amazing."

In that moment I have no idea what to say to him. I don't know whether to demand to know who had been fucking him, or yell at him for cheating on me and for letting someone fuck him bare. Or whether to tell him how confused I am right now, feeling so hurt by his betrayal but so aroused by it at the same time. In the end, after a silence that seems to last forever, all I can say is "I love you, babe."

CHAPTER 6
KENNETH

I hear Cole calling out something, but I can't make out the words over the sound of the shower. "What?" I yell back.

The bathroom door opens and Cole's head peers round. "Remember I'm home late," he says. "Going for a drink after work." He kisses me on the cheek. "Bye!"

"Have a good day, babe. Love you."

The door closes. I stick my hand under the water to check that it's hot enough, and then I jump into the shower.

It's about two minutes later that the bathroom door opens again. This time it's Josh, the next door neighbour, standing in the doorway. He saunters in, dropping his jeans and kicking them off. "Hey slut," he calls out over the sound of the water.

"Hey." As he's undressing I decide to give him something to look at. As obviously as I can I knock the soap off its shelf, turn around so my back is facing him, and bend over to pick it up, giving him a good view of my ass. By the time I straighten back up, he's opening the shower door behind me and stepping in.

He runs a hand over my ass, then gently up my hip and lower back. He leaves his hand lingering on the side of my rib cage, and takes a step closer so his chest and his cock —

already getting nice and thick — are pressed up against me. For a moment he just lets the jets of water fall across his face and his hair; then he starts to gently kiss the back of my neck.

I let out a sigh. Fuck, it drives me crazy when he kisses my neck like that.

"Glad you could make it," I whisper to him.

Josh's hand begins to travel again, this time making its way across my abs, up to my chest, then back down towards my hardening cock. But he stops short, teasing me by letting his hand linger on my groin, just above the base of my shaft.

I put my hands on the shower wall at shoulder height, to brace myself. I push my ass back, and rub it up and down against Josh's cock. His cock is now fully hard, and it doesn't take much convincing to get him to fuck me. He takes his cock in his hand and guides it slowly into my hole.

He wraps his arms around me, rubbing my chest and my torso as he begins to slowly ease his cock in and out of my ass. He nuzzles and kisses my neck and my collarbone, and runs his tongue slowly up my neck to my earlobe. Moaning with pleasure I push back into him, taking his cock a little bit deeper each time he pushes into me. "You like that, don't you?" he whispers, before taking my earlobe in his mouth and biting down softly.

"Yes. Fuck yes."

He takes me gently by the chin and turns my head so I'm craning my neck looking back towards him. He kisses me deeply, his warm, wet tongue filling my mouth and taking it over.

"I've got a late start today," he tells me, drawing his cock slowly out of me. "So we can take it slow." He slides it back in, right to the hilt.

He fucks me lazily for a few minutes, then pulls out. He grabs Cole's shampoo off the shelf and starts washing his hair. "I love the smell of this stuff, man," he tells me. "Way better than the shit I got at home."

While he washes his hair I get down on my knees. I lick his balls all over, as the warm water runs down his body and splashes over my face. He soaps down his muscular, hairy chest and arms while I service his ballsack. "Fuck that's nice," he sighs appreciatively.

Once he's done washing himself he says to me, "How 'bout we move this into the bedroom?"

That's all the encouragement I need. I turn the water off and step out of the shower. I grab a towel and dry myself off, and then hand the towel to Josh for him to do the same. It really gets me going the way his chest hair fluffs up when he dries it. I lean in, kiss his chest, his nipple. Lift his arm and kiss his pits. I love it when he fucks me in the shower; the only down side is that when he comes out his pits are clean and I don't get to smell that pure testosterone.

He finishes towelling himself off, and drops the towel on the floor. "Let's go." He slaps me on the ass.

We head into the bedroom, and we're barely in there before he throws me down on the bed, face down. I know the routine, and I know what Josh likes. So I get on all fours, ass up in the air, so he can get his face in nice and deep. He licks my freshly clean hole, getting his tongue in deep where his cock was a few minutes ago. Every now and then he runs his tongue down to my taint, which gives me the shivers.

It doesn't take him long to get worked up again. He flips me over. I instinctively bring my knees up to my chest. "You wanna fuck me now?" I ask him. Of course he does.

He spits on his hand, rubs it on his cock, and lines it up. With a slow, effortless stroke he slides it in deep, making me gasp. He pins me down underneath him and kisses me while he begins to slowly fuck me again.

I love my morning fucks with Josh. We have a good rhythm together after plenty of getting to know each other. He always looks deep in my eyes while he's inside me, kissing me all over my neck and my chest, holding me tight against him while he thrusts into me. This morning is no different. It's like it's not enough to just be inside of me; he pulls me so close, so tight that it's like he wants us to merge into one body or something. I love the intensity of it; he always fucks me slowly and gently - at least at first - but it still has this intensity like he's putting everything into that moment.

Eventually he steps up the pace. By this point we've both got a sheen on from the sweat, and I feel like I'm about to lose my shit from the way he's hitting my prostate slowly and rhythmically. He rises up so he's not pinning me down anymore; instead he's kneeling upright on the bed. He gets a good grip on my hips and starts to pound me hard. Every thrust his hitting my prostate; I feel that feeling like I'm about to piss myself, it's so fucking intense that I can't take it anymore. I let out a yelp as I suddenly cum. I feel my ass spasm and tighten around Josh's cock, as my own cock erupts and I blow my load all over my chest. The clenching of my ass sets Josh off too, and with a grunt I feel him unload inside of me.

He collapses on top of me, his chest heaving as he catches his breath. We both just lie there for a minute, and then he kisses me again.

He pulls out. He grabs the pillow and wipes his dick clean on it. He chuckles as he does it; he fucking loves that, he does it every time we fuck in our bed. He loves wiping his dick clean on Cole's pillow, knowing that my oblivious boyfriend is going to go to sleep with his face in Josh's dried up cum. He licks the cum off my chest, and then lies down next to me. "Thanks, bro. Needed that."

"You know it's here whenever you need it," I remind him.

He laughs. "I wish. If I could just come over and fuck you whenever I felt like it, I'd be over here a lot more often. Your boyfriend needs some new hobbies so you can get the house to yourself more often." He kisses me on the cheek, then the neck. "You know, he almost caught me on Tuesday."

"Really? You never mentioned it."

"I had other things on my mind." He grins at me. "Yeah, I was on my way over, thought he'd left already. Literally was just opening your gate when he opened the door and came out."

"What happened? What did he do?" The thought of him catching me is really fucking hot. Is that fucked up? Maybe it's fucked up. But I can't help it.

"Nothing. That dude is oblivious. I talked some shit, pretended I was on my way to the store so I ended up walking down the street with him. Then he went to catch the train and I came back here to pound the shit out of his slut boyfriend."

I could just imagine Josh's cocky grin, walking along talking to Cole like everything's totally normal, knowing that in half an hour's time he'd be wiping his dick clean on Cole's pillow. The thought of it starts to make me a little hard again.

"Do you ever worry he'll find out?" Josh asks.

I shake my head. "I don't worry. I know he'll find out at some point. It's only a matter of time. But I know Cole. I know he's a total cuck. So I know once he finds out I'm cheating on him it's gonna make him hornier than he's ever been before. So once he gets his head around it, he'll be glad I'm getting dicked down by guys like you."

Josh looks kind of confused. "A cuck? Like a cuckold?" I nod. "Like, you think he'll enjoy knowing that other guys are fucking you?"

"Yeah. Some guys are into it."

Josh looks incredulous. "Woah. I guess there's something for everyone. How do you know he's into it?"

"I don't know for sure. It's just a feeling. He's a sub deep down. And I see how turned on he gets when I tell him about all the guys that fucked me in the past. I mean, I don't know for sure. But I think I know him well enough to pick it."

"So why don't you tell him? If you think he's gonna be ok with me fucking you, wouldn't you rather just ask him than do it in secret?"

"I guess this way has advantages for both of us. I mean, maybe it's a dick move, but I love the thrill of fucking round behind his back. Once he knows, that feeling's all over for me, so I want to enjoy it while I can."

"And what's the advantage for him?"

I can't help but flash my most mischievous grin at that question. "Having a conversation about it is boring. But one day he's going to catch me in the act, and it is going to blow his mind."

CHAPTER 7
COLE

It's been almost two weeks, and I've been a mess the whole time. There are so many emotions, and questions, and thoughts, all flying around inside my head, and no way to resolve any of them. I'm so furious with Kenneth for cheating on me. But I'm even more angry at myself for being completely unable to bring it up with him. I should have said something when I'd first tasted some other guy's cum in his ass. I don't know why I didn't. In the days that have gone by since then there must have been a dozen times that I was bursting to say something to him, but every single time I couldn't bring myself to say a single word. He must know something's up; our conversations have been forced, distant. Like we're strangers. But I don't know where to even start.

What would I say? I want to yell at him, call him a fucking asshole and a slut. I want to tell him how angry it makes me that he would take another guy's load and risk giving me an STI. I want to tell him how much it hurts, the idea that he needs to get sex from someone else because I'm not enough for him.

But most of all I just want to know what he'd been doing. More than anything else I just want to pin him down and make him tell me how many men there have been, and what he'd let them do to him. Was there just one guy? Was he in love with someone else? I keep finding myself just staring off into space, imagining him with this unknown man. I picture them staring lovingly into each other's eyes, Kenneth saying to him "I'll leave Cole if you want me to." Or was it just a random? Was there a string of randoms, all lining up to take their turn on him? Did they all fuck him bareback? Did he kiss them, moan and whimper while they slowly fucked him? Did he beg them to cum inside him?

Every time I think about it - which seems like every second of every day - I feel sick to the stomach with dread. Each time my cock starts twitch and start to harden a bit when I imagine the details, and occasionally I knock one out while I imagine Kenneth getting his ass nailed by a faceless stud. And that just makes me feel even more confused. For a few minutes when I picture him being fucked I forget about the hurt, and just focus on every tiny detail of the sex I'm picturing. But as soon as I blow my load that sick, sinking feeling comes back, and I'm stuck with it.

I need to know. I need to see what he does when I'm not around. And I need to confront him with the knowledge of what he's done, and see how he reacts to being caught in the act.

And tonight's the night it's going to happen.

I came to the decision after only a few days, but it's been hard to find an opportunity to put the plan into action. I needed to have somewhere to go, that lasts long enough that Kenneth would be certain I'd be out for a decent amount of time. I needed to be able to give him some advance warning so he could make arrangements with whoever the guy was. And I needed to not actually be going anywhere, so I could come back to the house and catch him.

In the end I'd made up a fake dinner with some clients from work. When I'd told Kenneth a couple of nights ago he'd offered to come along. But I'd told him it would be long and boring and I didn't want to make him sit through it. He'd seemed okay with that. Ever since then it seemed like he'd been on his phone a fair bit; but I don't know if that's real or if I've just become hyper-focused on noticing every time he pulls out his phone in case he's talking to a hookup. I wish I knew his passcode so I could flick through and see the messages.

Tonight as I got ready I was nervous as hell. I was so tense, and my stomach was in knots. Hopefully Kenneth didn't pick up on it. I'd had a shower, and got dressed into some smart-casual clothes that would be suitable for the kind of dinner I was pretending to go to. I kept an eye out to see if Kenneth was on his phone, but there didn't seem to be anything out of the ordinary going on.

By now I'm a trembling, sweaty, nervous wreck. As the taxi toots its horn outside I give Kenneth a peck on the cheek.

"Have fun," he says.

"Thanks." My voice sounds like it's going to crack from the nerves. As I head out the door I remember to tell him, "Don't wait up, I'll probably be pretty late." Too obvious? I hope not.

I close the door behind me, and step out the gate to the waiting taxi. I climb into the taxi and the driver asks me where I'm going.

"Ah, just round the corner," I reply sheepishly.

"Just round the corner?"

"To the end of the street, and round the corner to the left." I feel so fucking stupid. "Sorry. I'll pay extra."

The driver looks at me and gives a wry smile. "You're the boss," he says.

Thirty seconds later he pulls up down the street and around the corner. I hand him a twenty and jump out. "Thanks," I say, embarrassed.

As the taxi drives off I start walking back towards my

place. It's getting dark so I figure I shouldn't have to worry too much about getting spotted, as long as I don't get too close to the house. There's a bus stop about five houses down from our house, so I stop and sit down there. I figure that if anyone saw me they'll assume I'm waiting for the bus.

I sit there for what seems like an eternity, my heart racing and my stomach flipping round like it's full of trapeze artists the whole time. Every time I check the time on my phone, only a minute or two has passed, even though it seems like I've been sitting there for hours. As I wait, all these thoughts play through my head - all these scenarios that could ruin my plan. What if Kenneth goes out to meet someone instead of inviting them to our place? I'd be screwed, because I wouldn't be able to follow. Or what if the person coming round is someone who knows me, and recognises me sitting here at the bus stop? I've been counting on the assumption that tonight will be the night I catch him in the act. If something screws up my plan, I don't know how much longer I can go without knowing what he's up to. God, this is agony. I just need something to happen so this can be over and done with.

But when something does finally happen it almost gives me heart palpitations. I see a guy - a fit, alpha-male looking guy — come round the corner and start walking down the street in my direction. Is this him? Or just some guy who happens to be walking down the street? But sure enough, when he gets to my house he stops and opens the gate. He walks up to the front door, and now I can't see him because my view is obstructed by the tree in our front garden. But I can hear him knock. Solidly. Confidently.

I can't see or hear what happens next. But I guess it's safe to assume I know what's going on.

Oh god, I think to myself. This is actually happening. What the fuck do I do now?

For a good minute or so I just sit there, heart pounding so hard I can hear it in my brain. I want to cry. I want to run away. But at the same time there's this longing so much more intense, to see what they're doing. So slowly I pick myself up off the bus stop bench, and walk towards our house.

I figure that it would take them a few minutes to get into it. Who knows, maybe they're going to sit around on the sofa with a glass of wine, talking about how great it is that I've got out of Kenneth's way so they can have the place to themselves. For a second I imagine them sitting there — this guy putting down his wine glass and leaning in, kissing Kenneth softly on the lips like I did on our first date.

I get close enough that I can see through the windows but they - hopefully - shouldn't be able to see me. But there's no sign of them. Does that mean they've already gone upstairs? I edge closer to the house, and then carefully unlatch the gate. Still no sign of them.

When I reach the front door the panic hits me like a wave. Am I really going to do this? Do I really want to see what they're doing? Wouldn't it be better just not to know? Does it even matter? Maybe I should just turn around, walk away and text Kenneth later to let him know our relationship is over.

But as I stand there at the door, the need to see him overwhelms me. I have to do this. I have to know what noises he makes, what faces he makes, and what words he whispers into the ears of this guy when they fuck in our bed.

I turn the doorknob ever so slowly. It's not locked so it opens easily. I push the door open the tiniest fraction, and listen. Silence. I push the door open a little bit further, and pause again. Again, silence. I slink through the door, turn, and push it shut behind me as gently as I possibly can. The door shuts with the tiniest click, but to me in that instant it sounds like a boom echoing in a cave. I freeze, and listen out for any sign that they had heard me come in. But there's nothing.

I peer round the door into the kitchen, but there's no sign of them. They must be upstairs. Holy fuck. Here goes.

I start to climb the stairs as slowly and as silently as I possibly can. Just in time I remember to step to the side on the fourth stair, to avoid the creak that it always makes when you step on it in the middle. As I climb I listen out, although it's almost impossible to hear anything over the rapid, booming heartbeat echoing in my skull.

Then I hear it. A long, deep sigh, coming from our bedroom. "Yeah. That's it."

My stomach lurches like I'm on a plane hitting turbulence. But I keep silently creeping up the stairs.

Our room is the furthest from the stairs. Closest is the spare bedroom, and between the two runs a large walk-in wardrobe with an entry from both bedrooms. That's where I'm headed; that's where I'm going to watch the action. As I reach the top of the stairs, I hurriedly creep along towards the spare room. Once inside, I let out a long, silent breath of relief, realising then how I've been holding my breath for the entire ascent of the stairs.

I hear a muffled moan. This time it's definitely Kenneth's voice.

The door to the wardrobe is already open, just as I left it. I creep in, and slowly edge my way forward without making a sound. Thank god we chose louvred doors for the wardrobe. Through the slats I can see right into our bedroom. There, I can see this alpha male from outside, standing naked in front of our bed. He has broad, muscular shoulders and a dusting of hair across his chest and abs, and has his head leaned back and eyes closed. Kenneth is on his knees in front of him, his head partially obscuring the well defined V of the guy's pelvic muscle as he slowly sucks his cock. As I watch, the stranger takes his hand and starts to gently stroke Kenneth's hair as his head bobs back and forth.

This is it. This is the moment I'd waited for.

I'm awash with all kinds of emotions. Anger's in there somewhere. But there's much more sadness than anger. I feel like my world is starting to crumble around me. And I feel my dick begin to swell.

Kenneth begins to go back and forth on the stranger's cock with greater and greater enthusiasm, and he moans with appreciation as he does. After a few times he goes real deep, and this time the guy grabs the back of his head and holds it in place, Kenneth's mouth right down to the hilt, until I can hear him start to choke and splutter. Then he lets go, and Kenneth pulls away with a gasp. For a moment I expect Kenneth to be angry at the guy for almost choking him, but instead he just gasps breathlessly and then takes the guy's cock just as deep again.

"Haha, you like that?" the guy teases with this arrogant, cocky smile.

"Yes," comes the reply, muffled by the cock in Kenneth's mouth. He takes it out, looks up at the guy and pleads, "Jake, fuck me."

Jake grins. "You wanna be fucked?" he asks, as if there was any ambiguity in the request. "I'll fuck you. Get on the bed."

Kenneth gets up and climbs onto the bed. It's then that I get my first proper look at Jake's cock. It's big — long, and wide, with a nice fat head that's glistening where Kenneth has just been sucking it. He has big, beautiful balls that hang heavy and full. It's an amazing sight. I'd already understood after seeing his muscular body and cocky smile why Kenneth would want him. But the sight of that big dick makes me properly understand what this guy can give Kenneth that I can't.

"How do you want me?" Kenneth asks.

"All fours."

Kenneth obediently gets on all fours, his ass facing in my direction. Jake comes up behind him and, without bothering to get a rubber on, shoves his dick into Kenneth's ass up to the hilt. Kenneth moans with what sounds like pain and delight. "There you go," Jake says, holding still with Kenneth impaled on the end of his mighty cock. "You've been wanting this dick haven't you?"

"So fucking bad," Kenneth replies.

"It's better than your boyfriend's baby dick then?"

I'm momentarily filled with rage, that he would even ask that. But when the reply comes: "So much better, your dick is amazing," the rage subsides, replaced with a sense of absolute shame. Suddenly I want nothing more than to be out of there, as far away as possible. I wonder what the fuck I'd been thinking. I'd been prepared for my boyfriend to be cheating on me, but I hadn't been prepared to hear firsthand him saying how inferior I was. I feel like I'm barely a few inches tall - like my whole body is smaller than the cock currently sitting half way up the man who was supposed to be mine.

I know I should leave. But I can't. Instead, I stand there transfixed as Jake slowly starts to pump his cock in and out of Kenneth's ass. Kenneth moans every time Jake drives his cock into him. Because of the angle all I can see is Jake's muscular back and ass as he pumps in and out, at first slowly and forcefully, but then sharper and faster. As he does Kenneth's moans become louder and higher pitched, becoming more like wails as his ass gets pounded from behind. Jake pulls out, then he gives Kenneth a forceful slap on the ass that makes him cry out. "Get on your back," he orders. Kenneth obediently complies. Then Jake slides his dick back in, leaning in to kiss Kenneth.

They fuck like that for some time. Jake stays bent over; I can hear him whispering into Kenneth's ear as they fuck but I can't make out what he's saying. Then Jake straightens up, grabs Kenneth's outstretched legs for grip, and starts really pounding him hard. "Fuck! Fuck!" Kenneth yells in time with Jake's thrusts. "Fuck yes. God that's good!"

I'm mesmerised by the sight of Kenneth getting fucked like that. And my cock is rock hard.

By now the bed's squeaking and rocking with the force of Jake's thrusts, and Kenneth's crying out to the same rhythm.

"How do you like that?" Jake grunts breathlessly as he fucks my man.

"Its... so... good..." Kenneth replies, each word escaping like a moan in time with Jake's dick driving into him.

"You want this cock? You want me to cum inside you?"

"So... much..."

"Beg for it."

"Please. Ahh. Please." The fucking gets faster and harder.

"You want my load?"

"Please! Yes! Fuck yes! I want... your cum... so bad!"

Fuck. They're getting close to the end. If I'm going to catch them in the act, now would have to be the time. I brace myself to push open the door. I have to. This is what I've waited for. This is what I need to do.

But I can't do it. I'm totally and utterly captivated watching them fuck. It's better than any porn I've ever seen. I'm so totally rock hard, as horny as I've ever been in my whole life, there's no way I can stop them now. I know I have to see this through. I need to see Jake cum in my boyfriend's ass.

"Fuck! Fuck!" Kenneth is practically screaming now.

"You're gonna take my load?" As if there was any question.

"Please! Breed me!"

"Does your boyfriend fuck you like this, slut?"

"Never! He could never... fuck me... like... this. God. Fuck. Fuck."

In that second, it's like the world is stood still. I see Jake's ass cheeks clench as he climaxes, and he lets out this low growl as his whole body spasms and he blows his load inside Kenneth. Kenneth lets out a moan of absolute bliss, and I'm pretty sure he's cumming too. And at that moment I reach down to fondle my rock hard cock, but before I can even touch it I feel that familiar surge of ejaculation flooding through me. It's unexpected, and uncontrollable. I feel my balls unload, and I blow a massive wad of cum in my pants. It keeps coming. Seven, eight times. It takes all the control I have not to cry out as I orgasm, and I can't help myself from gasping for breath.

I try to calm my breath, my cock still solid even after blowing my load. I look back through the slats, and see that Jake has collapsed on top of Kenneth and that they're passionately kissing each other. I feel a sting, knowing that I've never satisfied Kenneth the way this muscly alpha just has, and there's no way I ever would.

I slowly back out of the wardrobe. As I do I hear Kenneth say "Thanks, I needed that so fucking bad."

I creep out of the bedroom and back down the stairs, as quickly but stealthily as I can manage. I almost can't balance, my knees are so wobbly after the way I just came. But I get to the door, and hurry out and onto the street.

What the fuck now? The whole plan was to confront Kenneth and catch him red handed. Now I can't; I'm going to have to stay out and pretend I went to dinner after all. I start walking dejectedly down the street towards the local shops; I figure I could hang out at a cafe until it's late enough that I could have believably finished my work dinner.

When I get half way down the street my phone vibrates. I pull it out of my pocket. It's a message from Kenneth. It reads: *Did you like the show?*

All of a sudden I feel a sense of vertigo, like the earth has suddenly tilted sideways. The bottom drops out of my world again as I process the shock. He'd known I was watching the whole time. That motherfucker. How the hell did he know? He'd even belittled me, said that I couldn't fuck like Jake could. Right in front of my face. Did Jake know too? Are they

they both there right now, lying on my bed, laughing about how fucking lousy I am at keeping my own boyfriend satisfied?

I stand there trying to think of what to say in reply, but my mind is coming up blank. Then my phone vibrates again. This time it reads: *We're going to go another round or two. Would be good if you could stay out for a couple of hours at least. Thanks babe.*

As I read that message I feel my cock twitch. It reminds me about the wet, sticky feeling in my jocks. I look down. A patch in the front of my pants has gone dark where my cum has started to leak through. This is so fucking humiliating. For a moment I contemplate going back inside to grab a change of pants, or even to march back up the stairs and rip Kenneth to pieces for being such a cunt. But instead, I just carry on walking to the shops, adjusting myself in my cum-stained pants as I walk.

CHAPTER 8
KENNETH

That night with Jake couldn't have gone better if I'd planned it myself. As much as it turns me on having some sneaky sex on the down-low, for months now I'd been dying for Cole to find out about all the the guys who'd been fucking me behind his back. But as much as it turned me on thinking about the moment he caught on, and as much as I hated to admit, it I'd been incredibly anxious about how he'd react. Part of me always worried that as soon as he discovered what a cock whore I was, he'd dump my ass on the spot. I should have trusted my instincts though, because deep down I expected him to react just the way he did.

He'd stayed out till late just like I'd asked. I'd sent him a message later on that night to say that Jake had gone, and within about five minutes he'd been back in the front door. We hadn't talked that night, or fucked, or done much of anything, which was good because I was utterly spent. He'd just crawled into bed with this pitiful look on his face, kissed me and said "I love you." Then he settled into bed to sleep in the very spot where I'd just been bred three times by another man.

The following week or so though, there had been a lot of

talking. And I mean a lot. Cole had all these emotions he needed to put into words, and although I found it pretty fucking tedious I knew that the talking was necessary so he could get his head around it. Cole had told me about how hurt he'd been when he discovered I'd been fucking around on him, and how much of a fool it made him feel. He even raised his voice when he started on about how I'd been putting his life at risk getting fucked bare. He was somewhat placated when I assured him I was on PrEP, until I added that I'd been paying for it out of the joint bank account which was mostly his money.

He'd had a whole lot of anger and frustration to get out about the whole situation. But he'd also talked about how horny it made him. As if I hadn't figured that out from the cum stains on his pants when he'd come home that night. I was stoked that he'd found it so hot; that's exactly what I'd hoped for. "Even when Jake mocked you?" I asked him. "And when I told him he fucked better than you?" Cole had looked ashamed when he nodded.

I knew then that this was going to work out just the way I'd hoped. Cole wasn't quite as quick to see it though. As he worked through his emotions in a fucking painful amount of detail, he'd come to the conclusion that he was okay with an open relationship, but that we should start by playing together because he didn't like the idea of me messing around behind his back.

That's how we ended up here at the bathhouse tonight. He'd decided it would be a good way to road-test our newly open relationship; we'd be able to scout around, find someone we both liked, and play around together with a third.

I can see straight away this isn't going to turn out how he's expecting. I feel sorry for him, but at the same time I know it has to happen this way. And I can tell that even though it might hit him hard, he's going to be pleased in the end anyway.

It's not too busy at the bathhouse tonight, but busy enough. We've both had a shower, and we're having a bit of a wander round. Cole has never been here before so he wants to get the lay of the land; even though I know this place like the back of my hand I'm 'exploring' like I'm new to the place for his benefit. Cole is carefully attentive, studying the people, the rooms, the passages that lead off into the dark. I can see he's nervous, but he's trying to hide it by concentrating hard on taking in the surroundings.

It's not long at all before a couple of guys catch my eye, and I catch theirs. It never does take long. They eye me up, smile, and talk to each other in low voices without taking their eyes off me. One of them is blonde, with a smoothly shaved face and equally smooth and buttery skin on his muscular chest. The other is tall and slender, with sandy hair on his head, a dusting of golden hair on his chest, and a tiny golden trail leading down from his belly button, mostly hidden by his towel. Both of them look like they're in their mid twenties, cocky and confident.

The two of them casually saunter over.

"Hey," the blonde one says to me with a cheeky grin on his face.

"Hey yourself," I reply, flashing a smile at the pair of them. "How's your night?"

"Not bad. Been for a couple of drinks, thought we'd come chill for a bit."

There's an awkward pause for a second or two before the sandy-haired one adds, "Maybe you wanna come chill with us?"

I glance back at Cole, who is looking fully awkward, like he's not sure if he belongs in the conversation or not. I give him a questioning look, and he gives a small, curt nod.

I turn to the guys. "We'd be keen," I tell them. I gesture to Cole. "This is my boyfriend. We're playing together tonight. That ok?"

The guys study Cole for a second. "Yeah for sure, man," the blonde shrugs. He pushes open the nearest door and beckons for us to follow him in.

Once the door is shut behind us, the towels start to come off. The sandy-haired one goes straight for me, dropping his towel to the floor to reveal a long, uncut cock surrounded by shortly cropped golden hair like the stuff on his chest. He deftly removes my towel in a sweeping gesture, and takes a step forward so that our bodies are touching. He slowly, softly runs his hands over my ass as he leans in and kisses me. As his tongue pushes its way into my mouth, one hand runs its way up my back and settles on the back of my neck, while the other lingers on my ass. I put my hands around his hips and lean into the kiss.

I can feel my cock beginning to swell, and I can feel his begin to swell pressed up against me too. I reach for it, and ever so gently run my fingers up and down his shaft as it continues to get harder. The hand on my ass starts to slide down my ass crack, and he starts to apply the slightest amount of pressure to my hole as he begins to kiss me more passionately. I moan, and he starts to gently rub my hole as he grinds his stiff cock against my abs.

I break away from the kiss for a second, and look over at the other two. They're kissing each other, but both have their eyes firmly fixed on me and my partner. I shoot them a quick smile that's my attempt to be both reassuring to Cole and suggestive to the guy he's with. Then I kiss sandy-hair again, and start to work my way down his neck and chest with my tongue and my lips.

I kiss my way down his chest, pausing to lick and suck his nipples. I run my tongue along his abs and his pelvic muscle. As I do I bend further and further over, making sure to keep my legs straight so he can continue to reach my hole and keep massaging it with his finger. When I reach his dick I slowly take the whole thing in my mouth, and hold it there. "Fuck!" he sighs. "Fuck that's good bro!"

I take my mouth off his dick, and look up at him. He's grinning. "Don't stop man."

I take his dick in my mouth again, and this time I slide it the whole way in faster. I start to massage his balls as I slurp eagerly on his dick, while he moans his appreciation.

After a couple of minutes I hear, "Time to swap," and suddenly a second cock is in front of my face. I look up and the blonde is grinning down at me. "My turn. Have a taste of this." I greedily take this new dick in my mouth and go to work. He's cut and thick, with tight balls. After a few seconds of sucking I begin to taste the precum oozing out of it.

I feel the warm wet of a mouth sliding over my cock. I look down and see sandy-hair, starting to slowly suck me off. I look up, and I see Cole standing there, holding his erect cock in his hand, watching the three of us sucking each other off. After a minute or so, he nervously approaches the blonde and leans in to kiss him. The guy accepts his kiss, lingers for a few seconds, then turns his head slightly away to the side in a subtle indication to stop. Cole goes back to just standing there, slowly jerking his cock and watching us. "Come here and rim me," I offer, feeling a little sorry for him.

He enthusiastically obliges, getting down low so he can bury his face in my ass. I feel his warm, wet tongue start gently lapping at my hole. I go back to work on the big, thick cock in front of me.

After a few minutes the sandy-haired guy stops sucking my cock and climbs out from beneath me. The blonde leans back and lays down on the bed, so as I continue to suck him off I'm bent at a ninety degree angle. I hear "excuse me," from behind me, and feel Cole's tongue withdraw from my asshole and be replaced by a hard cock-head pushing up against it. I ease back slowly, my sloppy wet hole providing little resistance as it slowly slides inside me. I back up till it's all the way inside me, my ass pressing against his pelvis. I start to slowly buck back and forward on it, milking the cock with my ass.

"Fuck yeah, that's it," I hear the guy say behind me.

We continue like that for a while: me grinding slowly on the sandy-haired guy's dick while the blonde lies there letting me pleasure him with my mouth. Every now and then I look over at Cole; the look on his face is one of distress, but it's obvious that he's completely unable to look away or to stop stroking his hard-on which, by his standards, is massive by now.

After a while the blonde pulls himself up off the bed, careful to do it slowly enough that I can keep his cock in my mouth. Now both of the strangers are standing at either end of me, with me bent over between them. As they spit-roast me they begin to step up the intensity. The guy fucking me from behind stops letting me do all the work, instead starting to drive his cock into me harder and faster so I can feel his low-hanging balls slap against mine each time he gives me the length of his dick. As he does, the guy in my mouth takes hold of my head, and starts to face fuck me while holding my head in place.

"Fuck yeah. You like that?"

I'm not sure who's talking now, but it doesn't matter; whichever one of them is asking, I like what he's doing. "Yes," I mumble, my mouth full of cock and spit.

"You like watching your boyfriend get fucked from both ends?" the same voice asks. I don't hear a reply, so I turn my head as best I can to look in Cole's direction. He's jerking himself off faster now, that same pained expression on his face as when he climbed into bed next to me that night after Jake left.

The guys are really starting to work up a rhythm now, so that each of them drives their cock into me at the same time. It feels incredible, their cocks slamming into my mouth and ass simultaneously, then easing back, then slamming into me again. I feel like an accordion being played by their hard thrusting dicks. Both of the guys are moaning and grunting as they fuck me, and I realise at that point that I'm probably wailing like a little bitch. But I don't care. Fuck, they're giving it to me good.

The guy fucking my ass has built up to a frenzied pace, and I can feel his hip bones slam into my ass each time. "Fuck bro, I'm gonna cum," he warns. "You want my load?"

"Yes! Please!" I beg.

"Do you want me to give him my load?"

"Yes," I hear Cole's timid reply.

With that he lets out a long grunt and grabs my hips tightly as his cock spasms inside me. I feel his warm load fill me as he spasms again and again. "Oh fuck, that was good," he sighs.

He slowly withdraws his cock from my ass. The blonde withdraws from my mouth too, and the sandy-haired guy takes me by the hips and turns me round to face him. "You wanna clean me off?" he asks.

I bend over and greedily take his softening, but still engorged cock in my mouth, and start getting off every remaining bit of cum. At the same time I feel the blonde's cock start to push into me. This one, though not as long, is definitely fatter, and it makes me moan as it forces its way in. He doesn't waste any time going slowly or gently; he grabs me by the hips and starts pumping away. Meanwhile the cock in my mouth doesn't seem to be getting any more flaccid, so once I've cleaned the cum off I start to suck it and massage his balls with my hands. He responds pretty well, and before long his cock is fully hard again and he's facefucking me like his friend had been doing a minute or so earlier.

"It's a good hole, right?" the guy with his dick in my mouth asks his friend.

"Fuck yeah!" he exclaims, pumping my ass harder and

slapping me hard on the ass. I let out a little moan each time he slaps me. "Ha, he fucking loves it too. Don't you?"

"Yes," I mumble back at him.

"What's that? I can't hear you." He smacks my ass hard, making me yelp.

"Yes!" I yell out, still with the other guy's dick thrusting in and out of my mouth.

"I can see why. Look at what he's used to!" I don't need to look around to work out that me must be talking about Cole's dick.

The blonde grabs my hair from behind, and pulls my neck back. He uses it for leverage as he picks up the pace again, bucking into me hard. At the same time I feel a wad of cum hit me in the face as sandy-hair lets loose his second load of the night. "Oh yeah," he moans.

As I'm being nailed hard, the sandy-haired guy asks Cole "Want some cum for yourself?" Cole must have nodded because he then tells him, "Lick it off your boyfriend's face." A second later Cole's face is right there, a few centimetres from mine. He looks at me, unsure, questioning, like he's seeking permission. I nod to him, and he begins to tentatively lick the wads of cum off my face. It tickles a bit, but the hard pounding I'm getting in my ass distracts me from it.

When Cole finishes licking me he looks into my eyes, still with that same questioning, confused look on his face. I wonder what he's thinking; was it a look of why are you doing this to me? Or more a look of why do I love this so much? To reassure him I give him a long, passionate kiss. As I do I feel the guy in my ass pick up his pace a bit more, fucking me with quick, short, hard strokes. "You want this? You want my load?" he asks.

I break the kiss to answer "Yes!" emphatically. He grips my hips hard, and drives into me like a jackhammer. I look ahead into Cole's eyes, and smile mischievously at him as the guy unloads inside me with a low moan. I feel his dick throbbing inside me as it lets loose string after string of cum, and I let out a whimper.

The guy leans on my back, and keeps pumping slowly for another minute or so as his erection begins to subside. Then he slowly pulls out, and comes around to stand in front of me. He pushes Cole out of the way gently, puts his softening cock in front of my mouth, and looks at me expectantly. I understand the implicit instructions, and immediately begin to clean the cum off his dick with my tongue.

After I'm done, both guys put on their towels again. "Thanks man, that was fucking awesome," says the blonde who'd just been fucking me.

"Yeah, totally," the sandy-haired guy agrees. He turns to Cole. "Your boyfriend's got a great ass." He slaps said ass hard as the two of them casually walk out of the room, leaving me a sloppy, cum-filled mess lying on the vinyl-covered bench.

I look at Cole. The look on his face is intense. Shame, maybe? But what I'm not sure of is whether he's ashamed at how he'd stood there and let those guys fuck me like that, or whether he's ashamed at liking it.

"Do you want to fuck me?" I ask.

"No," he replies, looking at the floor.

"You sure?" I ask, grinning at him "I'm sure I can take another round."

He can't even look me in the eyes as he replies. "I can't. I already came. From watching."

"That's okay babe," I reassure him. "Did you have fun though?"

He still doesn't look at me, but he nods. "Yeah."

CHAPTER 9
COLE

The train stops, and the woman next to me gets up and disembarks. As soon as the seat next to me is empty, my phone's out and I'm flicking through cuckolding blogs looking for some new information I haven't read yet.

I've been completely consumed with a need to find out all I can about cuckolding. That night at the bathhouse was so intense — awful and sickening and magical at the same time. The rejection I'd felt when both those guys pretty much forgot about me, the awkwardness of standing there watching them take turns fucking my boyfriend from both ends. And the humiliation when they'd laughed at me and told me I couldn't satisfy Kenneth sexually. It runs through my mind constantly. I still can't understand why the humiliation turned me on so much. Fuck, when that guy let me lick his cum off Kenneth's face I could have shot my load in a heartbeat, if I hadn't already cum twice just from watching them fuck.

We hadn't talked about it for a few nights after that. It had taken me a while to process. I'd still been so ashamed by the whole thing, and so angry at myself for being so turned on by it. Kenneth hadn't said a thing about it; he just acted like the whole thing had never happened.

Finally, almost a week later, I'd mustered up the courage to have the conversation. I'd told him about how turned on I was, and how confused I was by my reaction to the experience.

Kenneth hadn't even seemed surprised. "I'm really glad that you enjoyed it," he'd told me. "To be honest, I just kinda knew you'd be into it once you tried it."

"What do you mean 'tried it?'" I'd asked. "I didn't do anything. I was supposed to join in, but you guys just kind of ignored me."

That's when he'd asked me if I knew what cuckolding was. I told him I didn't. I was sure I'd heard the word a few times, thrown around as an insult to guys whose wives were being fucked by other men. But beyond that I had no idea.

"It's when you get off on your partner having sex with other people," he told me. "It's when you get turned on, when you get sexual pleasure — not from being involved, but from being excluded. Watching the person you love get nailed by some other guy."

I scoffed at the thought. "What kind of guy would be into that?"

Kenneth had just looked at me while I let that question sink in. I was the kind of guy who'd be into that. Even though my rational brain was telling me that what had happened that night wasn't okay, and wasn't normal, I knew it had been one of the hottest experiences of my life. That night, and the night I'd caught him in the act at home.

"We know each other well," he'd said to me, reassuring me. "I just kinda had a feeling you'd love this. And I'm really excited you seem to have got so into it so fast."

"If you knew I'd be into it, why did you sneak around behind my back then?" I asked angrily.

"I know that was a shitty thing to do," he admitted. "I know you have a right to be angry with me about that. I guess the thing is, I knew you'd find out eventually no matter what

I did. And even though I know I'm going to enjoy cucking you, I also love the sneaking around. And I knew that once you found out, the sneaking around would be done for good. So I'm sorry, for being a dick, and not being honest with you. But I guess I kind of figured that I could have fun sneaking round for a while, and it would be hot for you to find out I was cheating."

He was right, I had to admit it. That moment I'd found out he was cheating was pretty goddamn hot.

We'd talked for a while about this whole new world, and it ended with me agreeing to go and read up on cuckolding to see what I thought of it. And as soon as I did, everything just seemed to click into place. Reading about other guys' experiences getting cucked by their boyfriends and husbands, seeing the judgement-free discussions online about why it was perfectly okay to feel the way I did. The feelings those guys described, they could have been writing about me.

Later that night, after getting horny as all hell reading stories about other guys' cuckold experiences online, I'd gone into the bedroom as hard as a rock and flipped Kenneth over. As I started to enter him he'd asked me, "So, think you're a cuck then?"

I almost came instantaneously when I replied "definitely." Luckily I held it together to avoid ejaculating then and there, because that night we ended up having some of the best sex we've ever had.

Ever since then I've been reading all about the lifestyle every chance I get. I've joined some forums, chatted to a few other cucks online and shared stories. As I sit on the train I reply to a couple of messages from other cuckold guys, one of whom is telling me that his husband is having a guy — a bull, they call them — over to stay the night in a few days' time. Reading the stories that cucks post online has become almost like an obsession to me. I just hope no one's reading over my shoulder as I sit there immersed in it.

As I jump off the train I get a message. It's a different guy from a gay cuckold chat group I've been talking with. He's messaged me to give me an update on the events of last night, when he went out to a bar with his boyfriend in the hope of finding a bull to bring home. Walking home from the train station we exchange messages, and he tells me that indeed they found a bull at the bar, and that he even got to watch his boyfriend and the bull make out on the crowded dance floor. I'm shook: the idea of doing that with Kenneth is a turn-on to be sure, but having your boyfriend humiliate you in public like that, it seemed like it could be crossing a line.

I don't know exactly what to say to this news, so I just reply, "Holy shit dude," as I step inside and put my bag down by the door.

"Hey babe, you home?" I call out.

There's no answer. I walk down the hallway into the kitchen, flipping through the mail to see what's in there. When I get to the kitchen though, I'm stopped in my tracks. The fridge door is open, and a naked figure is standing in front of it with his back to me. It's not Kenneth; his back is too broad and his legs too solid, and his hair is short and dark.

As I stand there he gulps down milk straight from the bottle. He finishes drinking, and wipes the milk moustache off as he casually turns round and looks at me. I can't help looking him up and down. He's got a big, uncut dick and low-hanging balls that he casually scratches as he stands there in front of me. His chest and torso are covered in closely cropped, dark hair; his body is solid but muscular, with big pecs and biceps.

"You must be the boyfriend," he says with a smirk.

It takes me a couple of seconds to react; I'm still a bit confused and distracted by this muscle stud standing in my kitchen. But I manage to get out the word "yeah."

He puts the milk bottle back in the fridge and shuts the door.

"Is Kenneth here?" I ask.

"Yeah of course," the guy replies. "He's still in bed." He walks out of the kitchen, me following behind. As he starts up the stairs he doesn't bother to turn back and look at me as he says, "I'd give us another hour or so."

I start to follow him up the stairs. "Do you think..." I ask nervously, "Do you think maybe I could watch?"

He gets to the top of the stairs and pauses outside my bedroom door, pondering the question for a moment. He looks me up and down.

"I won't try to get involved," I reassure him. "You don't need to touch me. I just like to watch, that's all."

He thinks about it for another second or so. Then he chuckles quietly. "Nah." He turns around and walks into the bedroom, kicking the door shut behind him.

For a second or two I'm fucking furious. I race up to the top of the stairs, and in my mind I'm thinking I'll barge in there and tell him *fuck you, if you're going to fuck in my bed then you're going to at least let me watch.* But by the time I reach the top of the stairs my rational brain has kicked in, and I know there's no way I'm going to do that. Instead I stand close to the door and listen.

All I can hear is mumbling as they talk to each other in low voices. I hear the two of them laugh, and I feel the humiliation stab at my guts as I wonder whether they were laughing about Kenneth's desperate boyfriend who begged to watch but got kicked out of his own bedroom.

I let myself slide down the wall till I'm sitting on the floor in the hallway, leaning against the wall next to the bedroom door. I desperately try to make out what they're saying, but all I can hear is mumbles and the occasional chuckle.

After a few minutes the talking stops, and all I hear is silence for a while. Part of me hopes that maybe they're just sitting in awkward silence, Kenneth trying to work out a way to politely indicate that the guy should leave. But I know that the silence is probably just because they've got their mouths full. After a while I start to hear the odd moan and whimper from Kenneth. I hear mumbling in a deep voice, which I'm guessing translates to something along the lines of "yeah, just like that."

By this stage my dick has been rock hard since the instant my bedroom door slammed shut. But now, hearing the sounds of him pleasuring Kenneth, I can't hold back any longer. I unzip my fly, take my erect penis out, and start to slowly stroke it as I listen to them making out and doing whatever it is they're doing in my bedroom.

Kenneth's moaning louder now. "Fuck," I hear him moan. "Fuck yeah, like that!" I hear the squelching, sticky sound of something I can't identify. Kissing? Jacking each other off? Fingers in Kenneth's ass? I have no idea. But Kenneth is moaning more and more insistently, till he cries out suddenly. That sound is instantly recognisable: the sound of him being entered, by something big.

"Fuck me!" I hear the dull thud of the bed taking the force of that stranger's fuck. At first it's just one thud. Then silence. Then another. The sound of a slow, intimate, but forceful fuck. With each thud, each penetration, Kenneth is gasping and moaning.

The pace gradually picks up, the thuds picking up a rhythm, the moans rising in pitch as they become more emphatic. I hear low-pitched grunts. "Yeah. Fuck yeah, take it."

"Fuck!" Thud. "Fuck!" Thud. "Arghh, holy..." Thud. "Holy fuck!" Thud. "Fuck me!" Thud. "God, fuck me!" Thud.

By this stage the bed is slamming against the headboard, and I can feel the wall vibrating against my back each time that man slams his cock into Kenneth. I look at the door, and I can see it quivering in it's frame, vibrating in time with the thuds as that guy slams my boyfriend's ass.

Kenneth's moans continue, but now they're muffled. Is the

guy kissing him while he's wailing from that fuck? Or does the guy have his hand over Kenneth's mouth while he's fucking him? Having to listen to this, having to imagine what they're doing because I can't see it with my own eyes, is agony. I'm picturing Kenneth face down on the bed, that bull pushing his face into the pillows while he pounds his ass from above. Kenneth's tight butt cheeks bouncing each time that man's body slams into them.

I can't take this any more.

I take my hand off my dick because I'm so close to shooting my load, but I don't want to do it yet. I want to last as long as they do. I want to cum hearing that stranger cum in Kenneth's ass, to have my release at the same moment he's having his. I sit on my hands to stop myself jerking off, and I just listen.

The thuds slow, just a little, but enough to notice. They're not so urgent now. It's like they're settling in to a leisurely rhythm, their bodies sychnronised with each other's. I imagine Kenneth looking back at this guy, a look of adoration in his eyes as the guy gets deeper inside him than I've ever been able to. I wonder how many times this guy has fucked Kenneth before, and whether Kenneth feels things for him when the two of them are fucking and they lock eyes with each other.

At that thought my hand goes instinctively back to my dick, and I'm jerking myself off again before I even realise it. I sit there on the floor, furiously jerking my cuck dick while I listen to the rhythmic creaking of the bed. I think back to the way the bull laughed at me when I asked if I could watch. The way he just dismissed me, before he shut me out of my own bedroom and claimed my partner in my own—

No, not yet!

I feel it course through me. I feel my dick pulse uncontrol-lably in my hand. I feel it all rush out, and suddenly I'm squirting all over the hallway floor. The orgasm makes me heave, and cry out. I jerk the last few drops out, and in an instant I feel exhausted, like I've just run a sprint.

I'm not sure, but I think maybe I hear quiet laughter from inside the bedroom. Maybe I'm just imagining it though. The creaks don't slow; the sounds don't change.

I know I should probably clean up, but I don't want to leave. I sit there on the floor, listening to the sound of them fucking, for maybe another twenty minutes or so. Slowly, each creak tells the story of a force that's pressing into my boyfriend and taking him over.

I feel ashamed when I realise they've probably now been going longer than I've ever lasted inside Kenneth. And I'm assuming this is their second fuck of the day, too. At least their second. When I realise that, my dick starts to get a little bit harder again. Maybe if I'm lucky I'll still be able to shoot a load at the same time the bull does.

Their fucking is getting faster. Kenneth's gasps are turning into moans again, getting louder and more pained as the fuck gets harder and more brutal. The thuds in the wall are getting louder as this bull slams my bed against it with every thrust of his big dick. They're getting faster — all the walls are shaking now like it's an earthquake. I look up above me and there's a picture shaking on its hook just a little.

"Fuck!" Kenneth is screaming. I grab my dick again and start jerking it off feverishly.

"Fuck!"

"You want it?" For the first time the bull yells out loud enough that I can hear the words clearly.

"Yes! Fuck! Cum in me! Please! Give me your load! Fuck! Fuck!"

The thuds are at jackhammer pace now, until suddenly the bull lets out a roar, and Kenneth lets out a wail, simultaneously. Then seconds later the thuds slow to a stop, as a few dribbles of cum drip from my dick as I ejaculate a second time.

I can hear the breathless breathing. A laugh. Muffled, hushed voices.

I continue to sit there in the hallway, bracing myself for the moment when the door opens, and they both look at me, judging me for being so pathetic. But nothing happens, other than that I can continue to hear the muffled noises of them talking, laughing, kissing.

Eventually I realise I've been sitting on the floor for close to an hour and a half. I get up, with pins and needles in my legs, and I head down to the kitchen to start cooking dinner. Twenty minutes or so later, I hear them come down the stairs and to the front door. Over the sound of pots cooking on the stove I can hear Kenneth saying goodbye "till next time", and the two of them kissing one more time. Then the door shuts, and the bull's gone.

Kenneth comes into the kitchen. He's naked, his hair tousled, looking exhausted. "Hey babe," he says, giving me a kiss on the cheek like it's any ordinary day and he's just got home. "Thanks for making dinner." He goes to the fridge and pulls out a bottle of water, gulping it down enthusiastically. Then, with a grin, he tells me, "I saw the puddle on the hallway floor. So, how many times did you cum listening to me take Ian's cock?"

CHAPTER 10
KENNETH

Cole's been fucking insufferable for the last week or so. I guess it's not like I can really blame him; he's been through a fair bit these last few weeks. I mean, finding out your boyfriend's been cheating on you — a lot — can't be easy I guess. And that night at the bathhouse was definitely pretty humiliating for him, despite how much he obviously loved it. He'd been totally warming up to the idea of being a cuckold though, until I went and pushed him a bit too far by having him come home to find Ian in the house. Maybe it wouldn't have made him so insecure if Ian had just let him watch. It was pretty funny though, and it made it pretty hot knowing that Cole was sitting outside in the hallway playing with his dick while he listened to me getting fucked.

Since then though, he's been so goddamn insecure. He keeps asking me where I'm going, whether I've been fucked that day. He won't let me out of his sight, either. And he keeps asking me if I still love him.

That makes me a little sad, to be honest. And it makes me feel like a dickhead for not showing him enough love. I've tried to be extra nice over the last couple of weeks. I make sure I tell him I love him, and that I'm grateful for him being cool about me having other guys on the side. And I keep telling him over and over again that I'm just doing it because it's hot, not because there's anything wrong with him or our relationship. I can see it makes him feel better. And it's true, of course. Every now and then though, I mention how all those other guys fuck me way better than he can. I can see him crumble a little, but I can also tell he loves it.

We've been fucking way more often lately. It always starts with him going down on me, while I tell him all about something I did with another guy behind his back. Pretty soon he's rearing to go and he jackhammer-fucks me; only problem is, though, that the stories get him going so hard that he usually blows his load after a few minutes.

Anyway, we've talked a bit about the whole thing. I've been pretty blunt and said that I'm going to fuck who I want, when I want, and he's not necessarily going to be around for it. He's fine with that. But I've also said that I'll try include him as much as I practically can, as long as the other guy is up for it. Tonight a guy called Ben's coming round to fuck me, and I've told Cole that he can be there for the whole thing. He's so nervous and excited, he's like a puppy or something. He's been wandering around the house, fidgeting, tidying, and constantly checking his phone for the time. It's been almost a month since he last saw me get fucked, so he's dying for it. Knowing Ben, though, Cole's going to get more than he bargained for.

It's almost nine, so Ben should be here any minute. "Babe, he should be here soon," I call down the stairs as I start undressing. "Can you let him in when he gets here?" I don't get a response, probably because Cole's completely losing his shit.

I dig around in my drawer to find my favourite jockstrap - one that Cole bought for me a few months back. It occurs to me that he's only seen me in it a couple of times, even though I actually use it at least once or twice a week.

I hear a knock at the door, and a few seconds later I hear Cole open it. I hear them talk briefly but I can't make out the words, and then I hear footsteps coming up the stairs. I get my jock on quickly, and get on the bed on all fours with my ass facing the door.

I hear them enter. "Nice," Ben says, obviously observing my waiting ass perfectly framed by the straps of my jock-strap. "This is what I like to see." He runs a hand over my ass, then slaps it playfully.

I hear the sound of Ben's belt unbuckling, and him removing his clothes.

"Where do you guys want me?" Cole asks. "Is there anything you want me to do?"

"Hmmm. Kenneth, any instructions for the cuck?"

"I don't care." I mean, it's not strictly true. I want to make this fun for him. And by fun I mean as humiliating as possible. But I figure the indifference is probably a good way to start.

"Ok." Ben is thinking for a second. "Cuck, I want you to to be able to see your boy's face. So you can see how he reacts having a real man give him what you can't. So get in font of him."

Cole comes round to the side of the bed and stands in front of me, a pained, nervous expression on his face.

"On your knees, dickhead."

Cole drops to his knees. His face is about at my level, only a couple of feet away. I can tell he's going to love this view.

"Babe, do I look good in the jock you bought me?" I whisper to Cole. I can't help smirking as I ask him.

"Of course, babe. It looks hot."

"How many guys do you think have had me wearing this jock, do you think?"

He doesn't answer, just looks stunned as the question sinks in.

"Ready, boy?" Ben asks.

"Of course."

"Ready to see how a real man treats your boy, cuck?"

Cole nods furiously. "Yes sir." He quickly corrects himself: "I mean, yes, I'm ready."

Ben and I both erupt with laughter at that. He's already turned into such a sub that he's calling my bulls 'sir' instinctively. He blushes from being laughed at, and he avoids looking either of us in the face.

I feel the bed move as Ben gets on it behind me. I feel his warm breath on my hole for a few seconds, and I shiver expectantly. Then I feel his tongue, so gentle it's barely perceptible, brushing over my waiting hole. I close my eyes, and let out the tiniest little sigh.

Ben starts to tongue my hole slow, gently, deliberately. He makes me wait between each stroke, so that each one catches me off guard and sends a shock through my body. I start to moan as the jolts course through my body.

Ben is such a pro at this. He goes on for what seems like forever; slowly building so that each brush of his tongue becomes a little bit firmer, and deeper, and lingers a little bit longer. I'm in fucking heaven. And each time I open my eyes, Cole's sitting there with this wounded, but utterly fascinated look on his face. I'd give him a grin or a cheeky wink or something if I wasn't so completely consumed by the feeling of Ben rimming me.

Eventually Ben stops. "This is getting me hard, boy," he tells me. "How 'bout you get over here and suck my cock for me."

I turn around to face him. He's in just his underwear, the outline of his thick, meaty cock straining to get out. He's so handsome. That thick, dark hair all over his chest and shoulders, disappearing into his briefs. His big, thick arms and wide shoulders, that look like they could pick me up and carry me as easy as a supermarket bag of potatoes. I smile at him. "Fuck, you're looking good daddy."

I gently reach in and take hold of his hard, heavy cock. I draw it out from beneath the fabric of his briefs, and hold it there for a few seconds, feeling the weight and the warmth of it. Then I bring my mouth to it and start to take it slowly in.

"Wait," Ben orders. I pause, not taking it in any deeper. "Cuck, get round here so you can get a good look."

I don't take my eyes off that cock, but I assume Cole's in place because Ben tells me to continue. I wrap my mouth around that cock and take it as far in as I can. Ben is so hung that I can't get it quite in balls deep, but close to. It fills every square inch of my mouth. I start to slowly go up and down on it, forming a tight vacuum to get some good pressure on it.

"That's it, boy," he tells me. "Fuck, you know I love how you suck my cock." I just mumble an "mmm" in agreement as I keep slobbering on it.

"Look how much he's enjoying it, cuck. Do you think he enjoys it this much when he's got your dick in your mouth?"

Silence.

"That wasn't a rhetorical question, shit-for-brains. Answer me. Do you think he enjoys it this much when he sucks your dick?"

"I don't... I don't know," Cole replies forlornly.

"Why don't we find out?" Ben puts a hand on the top of my head, and guides me off his cock. I look up at him. "Kenneth, who's cock do you enjoy more? Mine, or the cuck's?"

I open my mouth to answer, but Ben cuts me off. "Wait! Don't tell me. I have a better idea." He grins. "The cuck can get his dick out, and you can choose which one you want to suck on. Cuck, show us what you're packing."

Cole looks terrified for a second. Then he reaches down, undoes his fly, and pulls his cock out. It's fully hard, and it's been leaking already. Good sign; he must be enjoying this.

Ben erupts with laughter, pointing at Cole's significantly smaller penis. "What the fuck do you call that? Holy shit, now

I see why your boyfriend's always hitting me up to come give him a proper fucking."

Cole has gone so red, but his dick leaks a tiny little bit on hearing Ben say that to him.

"Hey cuck, let's compare. Let's put them side by side." He gets close to Cole, facing him so that their faces are only inches apart and their cocks are touching. "Tell me cuck, how do you think they compare?"

"Yours is bigger," he replies, with this resigned tone in his voice.

"Well of course mine's bigger. How much bigger?"

Cole seems tongue-tied.

"I want to hear you say it cuck. How much bigger is my dick?" As he asks his face gets real close to Cole's and he's staring him right in the eye.

Cole takes a deep breath. "It's at least about four or five inches longer than mine. And thicker. Like twice as thick."

"Good cuck. Now let's see which one your boyfriend wants."

He turns, so they're both facing me, holding their erect cocks in their hands. "You go for the one you want the most," Ben tells me.

I mean there's obviously no real choice, but I decide to draw it out for a few seconds as I survey them both. Then without a word I wrap my mouth around Ben's cock, maintaining eye contact with Cole the whole time. I look at him with glee while I gag on Ben's big, meaty cock. And Cole begins to stroke himself while he watches me go at it.

"Careful, cuck," Ben warns. "You don't want to set that thing off too soon. Nothing worse than having to watch me fuck your boyfriend when you've already cum. Trust me, it won't seem like so much fun after that."

Cole seems to pay attention to the advice; he keeps playing with himself but he slows it down, probably as slow as he can handle. I keep sucking on Ben's big dick till my jaw aches, looking up at Cole the whole time.

After a while, Ben stops me. "I think it's time for me to fuck you now, boy."

"Yes please."

"What does the cuck think? Do you want to see me fuck your boyfriend, cuck?"

Cole nods his head enthusiastically. "Fuck yes. So much."

Ben laughs. "That's what I like to hear." He tells me to turn around, facing away from him on all fours. And he orders Cole to get in front of me, on his knees like he was before.

"Now, cuck, you're gonna beg, aren't you."

"Beg?" Cole asks, sounding confused.

"Yes. Beg. Dumb cuck, is that too hard to understand?"

"Sorry." Cole gathers himself. "Please fuck him."

"For fuck's sake." Ben facepalms in frustration. "You can do better that that, can't you, dickhead?"

"Sorry," Cole apologises meekly. He tries again: "Please. Please, sir, fuck my boyfriend. I want to see you fuck him, please." He pauses, like he's not sure if he really wants to say what he's about to say. "I want to see a real man fuck my boyfriend, better than I can."

"That's better. Keep begging cuck."

"Sir, please take that huge dick of yours and put it inside Kenneth, further inside him than I can reach. I want to see you fuck him like I never could. Please fuck him, you deserve his ass more than I do."

"Get me some lube then."

Cole reaches for the bedside table and fumbles around in the draw. He pulls out a condom and a bottle of lube, and holds them out, offering them up.

Ben grabs the lube. "Look, baby," he says to me. "Cuck thinks I'm gonna wear a rubber."

Cole looks at me for my reaction. I give him nothing.

"I haven't worn a rubber with your boyfriend yet, cuck, and I'm not planning on starting today."

Cole doesn't argue.

"You don't want me to, either, do you?" Ben kept pressing him. "You want to see Kenneth take my load, don't you cuck?"

Cole's silent.

"Don't you, cuck?"

Cole nods, not making eye contact. "Yeah."

"Yeah what?"

"Yes sir. I want to see you cum inside Kenneth."

That makes me smile. "Love you," I whisper to Cole.

I hear Ben lube up his cock, and then I feel his lube-covered fingers exploring my hole. He pushes a couple of them all the way in, getting it loose, all nice and slicked up, ready for his cock.

I study Cole's face, as Ben's fingers massage my prostate, making me shudder. Cole's eyes flicker from my face, to Ben's, and back to mine. I can tell he's torn because he wants to look at my reaction, but at the same time he's desperate to see what Ben's doing to my ass.

"You ready, cuck?"

Cole looks at Ben. Then he looks at me. Wide-eyed. Confused. Totally immersed in the moment.

"Yes."

I feel the bulk of Ben's cock pushing against my hole, and I feel my hole start to give way to it. It slowly slides in, stretching me out. Ben lets out a sigh of pleasure as he pushes it slowly all the way in, until it's filling me up completely. He draws it out, and when he slowly pushes it all the way back in I'm in ecstasy. I let out a little whimper and I close my eyes, concentrating on the feeling of his dick sliding slowly in and out of me.

For a moment I forget everything else in the world, I'm so lost in the pleasure of being fucked. Then I open my eyes and see Cole's dejected look. In that moment I know exactly what he's thinking: he can never make me feel that good. I like it when he fucks me, but I never lose myself with him the way I lose myself with a hung alpha male. He sees the look on my face and he knows that he's never been able to make me feel like I do right now.

Ben picks up the pace. He grabs the waistband of my jockstrap like a rein, and starts to hammer my ass. I let wave after wave of pleasure sweep over me. I know that I must have the biggest, blissed-out grin on my face right now — not even on purpose to humiliate Cole, but because I just can't help myself. I know it must be fucking with him though, because every time I remember to open my eyes for a second or so he looks completely stunned. He's just kneeling there, dick in hand, his eyes flickering from my face to Ben's as we fuck.

He fucks me from behind for ages. Cole's never lasted this long.

I decide to send my boyfriend over the edge. "Come here," I whisper to him.

He edges closer to me, his face just inches from mine.

Ben rams his dick in really hard; it makes me wince, and let out a moan. I feel a bead of sweat drip down my face.

"Kiss me, babe."

Cole looks confused, and stays still. But I give him a nod, letting him know it's ok. He leans in, and kisses me. Then he pulls away, so his face is still right there, close enough that he can probably feel my breath on his face as I pant.

I whisper quietly to him: "the best fuck you've ever given me doesn't even come close to how good it feels to have Ben's cock inside me right now."

Cole lets out a wail, like an animal in pain. He closes his eyes, and his face contorts. When he opens them, he looks down, and then looks back at me, ashamed. I look down and see his hand covered in a thick wad of cum, his dick still pulsing out the last little dribble.

I chuckle.

Ben notices too. "Blow your load, did you, cuck?"

Cole just nods.

"That's a shame. Because I've still got a long way to go, and now you're gonna have to sit there for the whole thing without your little hard-on to entertain you." He slows down his fuck, and lays down on top of me, so I can feel his breath on my ear, and his face is now only inches from Cole's.

He whispers in my ear, loud enough for Cole to hear. "You glad you're getting my load and not his second-rate cum, baby?"

I nod. "Yeah, daddy."

Now that Cole's cum, we ignore him for a while. Ben bites my ear softly, and we make out while he fucks me with long, slow strokes. He flips me over onto my back, and puts himself back inside me missionary. Our bodies pressed hard together, we make out wildly. Ben knows exactly where on my neck I like to be bitten and kissed, and he lingers around there as he explores my body between kisses.

We've been at it for ages now, and I can feel my jockstrap is soaked from sweat and precum. I look over at Cole for the first time in a while, and I see that he's holding his semi-erect cock in his hand again. I grin at him.

Ben puts my legs up in the air and starts pounding me harder. I can't help but cry out each time his big dick slams into me. I can tell he's getting close now.

"I'm gonna cum, baby," he tells me.

"Fuck daddy, please!"

He's pounding me even harder, his balls slapping against my ass cheeks with each thrust. I close my eyes and focus on the sensation.

"You ready to watch me breed your boyfriend?" Ben asks.

"Yes."

"You gotta beg, cuck."

"Please cum in him. He deserves your load. Please."

Fuck he's pathetic.

"Breed me, daddy!" I beg.

With a roar, he gives me his hardest thrust yet as he buries his dick deep inside me and lets his seed loose. I can feel his cock pulsing, and I can feel his cum fill me. For a moment everything else disappears, all I experience is the darkness and the sensation of his powerful seed filling me. Then, as the seconds go by, I start to notice the rest of my body again. I feel the sweat on my face, my pounding heartbeat, the ache in my legs from being pushed up against my chest for so long. I hear Ben's heavy breaths. I open my eyes and look at him. He's panting, his chest heaving. Sweat's rolling down his forehead, making his dark skin glisten. He grins at me for a few seconds, and then I feel him pull out of me. He rolls over onto his back beside me.

I look over at Cole and see that he's shot a second load into his hand. He looks shellshocked.

"Get us a towel, cuck," Ben orders. Cole quickly jumps up and runs out of the room, returning a few seconds later with a hand towel. He hands it gingerly to Ben, who first uses it to wipe the sweat from his brow, and then the cum from his dick. He hands it to me and I wipe my ass, which is already leaking cum all over the sheets.

I look at Cole. "Did you like that, Babe?"

He nods enthusiastically, still looking traumatised though. "Thanks for letting me watch."

"Its fine babe. I really enjoyed it. Now, if you give me and Ben a little bit of alone time, I'll let you lick his load out of my ass after he leaves."

Cole's eyes widen. "Ok, yeah, definitely. How long do you need?"

"We'll be done when we're done," Ben interjects. "Now get the fuck out. And close the door after you."

Cole does what he says. With the door shut, Ben and I are alone to make out and cuddle for a bit. But it cracks me up knowing Cole will be sitting there right outside the door.

CHAPTER 11
COLE

Today's my thirty-fifth birthday. It's been nice; Kenneth and I had lunch with Ewan, my best friend going back decades who I don't see all that often. Later we spent some time wandering around town so I could pick out some clothes for Kenneth to buy me as a birthday present, because he's terrible at choosing stuff himself. To be honest, after all the crazy shit that's been happening the last couple of months, it's kind of been a welcome change to just do some ordinary couple stuff together.

All day though, Kenneth has kept telling me that he's got some kind of surprise planned for tonight, but he won't give me any hints about what it is. Generally speaking I'm not really one for surprises, but I figure it's nice of him to have gone to the trouble, whatever it is.

It's after seven, and we're on our way home. Seeing as how Kenneth insisted we stopped in at the supermarket for a bunch of groceries that didn't seem that urgent, I'm suspecting that his surprise is probably a party at our house and he's filling in time to allow for people to arrive. I'm guessing that there are a bunch of people turning up at our place at the moment, getting ready to jump out and yell "surprise" at me when I walk through the door.

I try prod him about it again. "So you're really not going to give me any clues at all?" I ask, for about the fourth time today.

"Nope. Nothing." He looks at me with a mischievous glint in his eye. "I bet you'll love it though. And I bet you will be properly surprised."

We pull up to the house, and I can see there are lights on inside. I figure that's a little poorly done; they're supposed to wait in the dark so I don't expect it, aren't they? But I figure I'll just act oblivious and pretend I don't notice the lights.

I walk up to the front door, bracing myself for my best attempt at looking surprised. I open the door, and, sure enough, the house is full of people standing around, drinking. There's Adam and Paul, James, Charlie and Luca, a couple of guys from work, Josh from next door, one guy who I can't place at all. Ewan is there too, having kept quiet about it the whole time we hung out a few hours ago. As they see me enter a few of the guys raise a glass, and I hear a few hoots and cheers. Someone says, "Here's the birthday boy!"

The reception seems a little underwhelming for a surprise party. But I put on my best attempt at a shocked face. "Whoa! Surprise party?" I turn and look at Kenneth. "Thanks hun, I'm guessing this was your doing?"

Kenneth chuckles and shakes his head. "This isn't the surprise, babe."

"Oh?" Now I am legitimately a little surprised. "What —"

Kenneth cuts me off. "You're just gonna have to wait. I promise, it'll be epic."

James saunters over and puts his hand on my shoulder. "We're all pretty amped for it," he tells me, with his trademark arrogant smirk. He takes me by the shoulders and leads me through the lounge towards the kitchen, and the drinks. "Come on, birthday boy. Let's get some drinks in you."

As James mixes me a rum and coke, the guys come over one by one to wish me happy birthday. Paul gives me a hug, and Adam jabs me in the ribs. "Happy birthday, old man," he says.

"Ha. I may be old, but no matter how old I get I'll never be as old as you."

Ewan comes over and grips me in a one-armed, straight guy kind of hug. "Happy birthday, bro."

"You kept this to yourself!"

He laughs. "I didn't want to ruin your surprise."

As I stand there chatting to the guys in the kitchen, Kenneth sidles up to me. He leans in, and in a hushed voice he says to me, "I've got a secret to tell you. Someone at this party has fucked me."

"What the —?" I scan the room, wild-eyed. "Who?"

He laughs and shakes his head. "Not telling. It's more fun this way."

From that point on I can't shake the thought. For the next hour or so I'm watching everyone like a hawk, looking for any telltale signs that one of the guys at the party has a more familiar relationship with Kenneth than they're letting on. It's hard though — the more I watch, the more I realise that just about every guy in the room acts kind of flirty when they talk to him. Knowing grins, casual touches — it's like every guy in the room is hitting on him. The thought that someone in this room has fucked Kenneth behind my back is both embarrassing and hot. I wonder if they laugh at me behind my back for being so oblivious to it.

A couple of hours into the party, and Kenneth's promised surprise hasn't eventuated. I'm starting to wonder if maybe his revelation before was the surprise. I mean, it was a bit of a bombshell, and it definitely turned me on. I figure there must be more though.

It's about nine when Kenneth clears his throat to get the attention of the room. "I think it's time for the main event!" he proclaims, to a round of cheers from everyone present. He grabs a chair from around the dining table, and sets it down in the middle of the room. "Take a seat," he tells me, nodding towards it.

I look at him hesitantly, but his face gives nothing away. So I take a seat in the chair. "Now what?" I ask, looking around at all the guys, who have started to gather around me.

Suddenly I feel something cold against my wrist. I look down, and see a leather cuff being attached. I look up, and Paul is grinning at me as he locks the restraint and attaches the other end of the chain to the arm of the chair.

"What the..." As I mutter the words I feel another cuff go onto my other wrist. I look around and see Adam clipping the other end to the chair arm.

"Guys?"

Then they're cuffing my legs. For a moment I start to feel a mild sense of panic, but then I figure I should just go along with it. It's just the kind of tomfoolery I should have expected from this lot. With a laugh that sounds a bit more nervous than intended, I say, "Guys, I didn't know it was going to be this kind of party!"

That gets a laugh from the group, with a few of them exchanging knowing glances. When the laughter has died down, Kenneth raises his hand up into the air as a cue for quiet.

"So," he says, looking round at all the guys in the room, "I promised Cole a surprise for his birthday, and I'd like to start by thanking you all for helping out." There's a few sniggers from around the room. Then he looks straight at me, while still addressing the party. "Most of you know by now, that my kind, loving, boyfriend Cole..." He winks at me "... is a cuckold, who loves it when I give my ass up to other guys."

Holy shit.

What the fuck is he doing? In front of all these people?

Fuck, there are guys from my work here, and most of my closest friends!

"But what Cole doesn't know, is just how many of his friends have had his boyfriend's ass."

There's a second of silence as everyone in the room looks at me to gauge my reaction.

"Kenneth, what…" I feel like I need to stop this, before it goes too far. Hell, it's obviously gone way too far already.

"So, who's gonna get the ball rolling?" He looks around, and in that moment of silence I can hear my heart pounding in my chest.

Then Paul speaks up. "I'll start," he says with a grin. "Cole, do you remember that pride party about a year back? The one where you went home early and we stayed out?"

I swallow. "Yeah."

"You remember how Kenneth crashed at our place, right? Well, I guess he never told you about how he started grinding up on me in the bar, sliding his hands up my shirt, telling me he wanted my cock? And how Adam and I took him home, and fucked him all night?"

At this moment I have no idea what to say. Then Adam pipes up. "And again the next morning. I reckon we probably fucked about eight loads into him between us before we dropped him back at your place."

"Since then we've probably fucked him dozens of times each," Paul continues. "Like at my birthday party a few weeks back. And the next day when he came to pick up the car. Oh, and that time you passed out drunk on my sofa? He sucked our cocks right there next to you while you were sleeping, then we took him upstairs and fucked him. We got both our cocks in him at once."

That last remark gets a few appreciative whistles and hollers from the group. I just look at the floor. What the hell am I supposed to say to that?

"My turn!" James says gleefully. "I've fucked Kenneth a

couple of times. There was Paul and Adam's party, that time at the bar, that night we all went out for dinner…" He stops to think for a second. "Oh, and that time I saw you at the bus stop and gave you a lift to work," he laughs. "Fuck, Cole, your boyfriend has the hottest ass in town, and the easiest."

Everyone laughs, and a couple of guys murmur their agreement. Kenneth throws up his hands in mock modesty. "So nice of you to say, James." He looks over at me. "Hey baby, you enjoying this?"

I look him straight in the eye. I try to glower, to burn a hole into him with the ferocity of all the humiliation I'm feeling. But I know that it's coming across as something pitiful. And I have to admit to myself that the scowl is really just a performance of how I think I should be feeling, because where there should be anger there's only arousal.

"He must be enjoying it," Charlie chuckles, pointing at me. I can see his cock trying to get hard in his pants!"

"No way!" Kenneth exclaims. "That's awesome baby!" He comes over to me, kisses me on the lips, and starts to unbuckle my belt. "We should get it out so everyone can see!"

"Kenneth, no!" I try to struggle. I can move each limb a few inches with the length of the chains but it does no good. "Please!"

He pauses. 'You want me to stop? I just want everyone to see how excited it gets you when you hear about them fucking me."

I pause. It's embarrassing, for sure. But the embarrassment kind of has a thrill of its own, and I kind of want it to continue. I say nothing, but I give him a little nod.

Kenneth unzips my jeans and grabs my cock. Up until a few seconds ago I hadn't even noticed it was hard. He pulls it out of my trunks and leaves it sticking out for everyone to see. "Check it out guys, see I told you he'd love it!"

With that there are hoots and hollers of laughter.

"Woah Kenneth, I can see why you need so much cock on the side," James says. "What's a dick like that gonna do?"

"Hey, be nice to Cole man!" Adam says, coming to my rescue. "It's his birthday, remember?" He puts a hand on my shoulder and tousles my hair. "Anyway, who's next?"

It's Josh's turn. "I breed Kenneth most mornings in the shower after you leave for work," he tells me. "Oh, and thanks for letting me use your shampoo and cologne while I'm there."

Howls of laughter again. This is so humiliating I can't bear it. But I feel my cock twitch.

"My turn," says Joseph, the guy I just met earlier tonight. Of course this guy's fucked him too. Now it makes sense why he's at the party. "I met Kenneth about a week ago, on a plane. I fucked him in a stall in the airport toilets. Then I took him home and fucked him a few more times there." He says it so matter-of-factly, like he's talking about a bottle of liquor he bought duty free.

Someone inhales as though they're about to launch into their story, but Joseph carries on: "Then he came back the following night and I fucked him a couple more times. Then a couple more the following morning."

That one hurts. God damn. He stayed over at this guy's place when he told me his flight had been cancelled. And then he went straight back the next day?

Surely it can't get any worse than this.

How wrong am I, because Ewan's the next one to pipe up. "I fucked Kenny a while back, when I came round to the house to borrow Cole's sander."

"What the fuck Kenneth! My best friend?" And all these years I thought the guy was straight, too. I can't fucking believe this. I can feel my whole face burning, from rage, or shame, or both.

"Look Cole," Ewan says, looking at me with pity in his eyes. "I felt fucking terrible about it. I mean, fucking your best friend's boyfriend is pretty much the worst thing a guy can do."

There's not a sound from around the room as he pauses; the mood suddenly seems to have shifted awkward for everyone, not just for me. But then he looks over at Kenneth, and flashes a cheeky grin. "But Kenny was wearing those slutty shorts and he was just begging for my cock, and his ass felt so good. And man he rode my cock like a fucking bronco. So of course I had to go back for it a few more times."

That gets a cheer. Kenneth shoots Ewan an annoyed look though. "You know I fucking hate it when you call me Kenny."

"Haha, you love it when I call you my bitch though, right? We fucked on your bed a couple of times," he carries on. "Oh yeah, and you know that guy he stood you up for about two weeks ago? That was me."

At this point all I can do is hang my head. But my cock is raging, and when I look down I can see it's leaking.

I start to go into a daze so I don't even fully catch the next few. But Shaun from work says that he fucked Kenneth at some work function, and Luca tells everyone about how he came round and fucked Kenneth in our bed one time. Which gets a "me too!" from Brett, who adds "I nutted all over your sheets, bro!"

At this point it sounds like everyone's done. Except Ryan, who says, "I guess I'm the only one here who hasn't fucked Kenneth. But I'm mad keen to."

"That sounds like a good segue," Kenneth says with a grin. "Time for the next bit of the surprise I think! Who's up?"

Suddenly there's a clamour as about five guys all volunteer to be first. But Paul cuts through the noise: "I think the birthday boy should get to decide, right?"

"Decide what?" I ask. It's pretty obvious what they're talking about though.

"Who do you want to fuck your boy first?"

I look around the room. I can feel tears welling up in my eyes. I can't believe this is happening. I shut my eyes tight, and some part of me wishes that this was all over. But in my mind's eye I can see all these images of my friends fucking Kenneth. And they are all so god damn hot that it makes me want to blow my load right there and then.

I open my eyes and look around. "Ryan." I look at him. "You're the only one who's missed out so far, so you should get to go first."

I look over at Kenneth, and he's got the most massive grin on his face I've ever seen.

Ryan looks a bit hesitant. "You sure?" he asks me.

I take a moment to really think about my reply. I look around the room, and think of the utter degradation of having my friends claim my boyfriend in front of me. I look at Ryan, and wonder what he fucks like, and what he can do to Kenneth that I can't. And I know with complete certainty that I want this to happen.

"Yes. I want you to fuck Kenneth."

The room erupts in cheers.

Ryan still seems a little hesitant at first, but with a bit of encouragement from the other guys in the room he walks over to Kenneth, places a hand on his hip, and kisses him. At first it's gentle, but it quickly becomes more intense. Ryan places his other hand on Kenneth's back, and they make out eagerly and messily like a drunk couple in a nightclub. James is behind Kenneth, unbuckling his belt and then slowly pulling his jeans down to reveal Kenneth's firm ass neatly packaged by a black jockstrap. Another one that I bought him, but very rarely get to see him in. Kenneth takes Ryan's hand and slides it down to his ass, and Ryan grabs it firmly.

They make out for a few more seconds, then they move to the sofa. Ryan lays Kenneth down gently, and starts to undo the button fly on his jeans as he kisses his neck. Then he's on top of him, pants around his ankles while Kenneth wraps his legs around him.

Kenneth looks straight at me, then whispers audibly in Ryan's ear "Fuck me."

That's all the encouragement Ryan needs. Seemingly out of nowhere Paul's there to offer him some lube. He squeezes a bit out, rubs it all over his cock, and then slowly slides into Kenneth's ass right there on the sofa. Kenneth lets out a moan, and the watching crowd whoop enthusiastically. Ryan starts fucking Kenneth slowly.

Even though Ryan's obviously enjoying the feeling of being inside Kenneth, I can tell he feels a little bit awkward about fucking him right in front of me. He doesn't make eye contact with me at all as he slowly slides his cock in and out of Kenneth's ass. Kenneth, on the other hand, looks right at me as he takes Ryan. "Babe, it feels so good!"

I can't believe he would humiliate me like this in front of everybody I know. I can't believe that he's cucking me right there with all my friends watching. It hurts so hard, knowing that I've lost the respect of everyone in the room. But the mental hurt goes hand-in-hand with the pain of my cock straining so hard that it's aching. And I remember that some kinds of hurt can feel pretty good.

"Babe," Kenneth asks me, "Do you like watching him fuck me?"

Ryan looks up, looks at me for the first time. I can see in his face that he's worried about what I'm going to say. He's worried that he's gone and pushed the joke too far, and done something he can't take back.

I nod. "Of course," I tell them.

Ryan looks relieved.

"Babe, give Ryan a bit of encouragement, will you?"

Ryan looks a little alarmed at that. Suddenly all eyes are on me.

I panic for a second. What do I say? I stammer, "Thanks for fucking him, Ryan."

There's a few laughs.

"You're gonna breed him, right?"

Ryan's worried face breaks into a grin. "I'm sure I can do that for you, man." He sticks his tongue in Kenneth's mouth and starts to fuck him harder. He lifts Kenneth's ankles up around his neck, and puts the full weight of his hips on Kenneth as he drives his cock into him. The others start to chant in times with Ryan's thrusts and Kenneth's moans. "Fuck, him, fuck him!"

Now he's properly getting into it. "Your boyfriend's got a tight ass for someone who gets fucked so often," he says, turning to look at me for a second.

He picks up the pace some more. The chants are getting faster, and Kenneth's moans are getting louder and breathier. It's obvious Ryan's close to cumming. He drives his dick in hard, leans in and makes out with Kenneth some more. A few of the guys start a kind of drum-roll, banging on the furniture, letting out a low "ohhhhhh" that rises in pitch as the fucking gets more intense. Then with a final hard, deep thrust, he cums. The group erupt into a cheer as they see Ryan's face contort and his body clench up. It's so goddamn hot to see my workmate release his load into Kenneth, surrounded by a room of my friends cheering him on.

After a few seconds Ryan pulls out, his cock slick with cum. He looks up, gives the room a grin and asks, "Who's next?"

"My turn!" Paul jumps in, before anyone else can volunteer. "You want me to show you what I've been getting up to with your boy, cuck?"

God yes. I've always wanted to see Paul fuck. That muscular body. The stories I've heard about him over the years. I've always known Paul was one hundred percent alpha to my half-hearted beta. "Yeah, get in there," I tell him.

"You gotta ask nice though, cuck." Fuck, he's loving this. I never realised that Paul had the desire to degrade me like this.

"Please fuck him," I beg. "I want to see how you fuck him."

He laughs. "Happy to oblige." He starts to undress. I've seen Paul's bulge before, so I know he's hung. But when he takes out his cock I can see that it puts mine to shame. "Okay cuck, get ready to see what your boyfriend's really wishing for when you're fucking him."

He sits down on the sofa, directly facing me. Kenneth gets on his lap, his back to me. They make out, and it's obvious they know what each other likes. As they kiss, I can see Paul's cock get harder and thicker, and Kenneth begins to stroke it to its full size. Once it's ready, he slowly lowers his ass down onto Paul's shaft. From this angle I get a full view of Paul's cock being engulfed by Kenneth's hole, stretching it out. Kenneth lets out a satisfied sigh as it fills him up.

I'm so transfixed that I barely notice the voice talking to me. I snap out of it and look up. It's Luca. "You still ok, man?" I can see the look of sympathy in his eyes.

"Fuck yeah. I'm good." I turn back and ignore him, completely captivated by the view of Paul's big, thick dick sliding in and out of Kenneth's hole.

I have no idea how long they go on like this. If it had been porn I probably would have got bored by now and skipped to the money shot. But the sight of that slick, wet, bare cock entering Kenneth over and over again, it has an effect on me I can't begin to explain. It mesmerises me completely. The two of them are lost in each other, joined at the mouth. But every minute or so Paul pulls away, and locks his eyes directly on me for a few seconds. He just sits there, this smug grin on his face, while Kenneth slowly rides him.

Eventually Adam demands to be let in on the fun. Paul and Kenneth get up off the sofa, and Paul tells Kenneth to get on his hands and knees on the floor. Then he slides his cock back in from behind him, while Adam gets down on his knees in front of Kenneth's face. Adam offers up his cock, and Kenneth takes it greedily in his mouth.

"Your boy's one of the best cocksuckers I know," Adam tells me, closing his eyes and leaning his head back.

"And he's got one of the best asses I've ever seen," Paul chimes in. "You know we fuck a lot of guys, right? But Kenneth's always first choice."

"How many times?" I ask nervously.

I can see Kenneth laughing at the question, despite having his face full of cock.

I can see Adam trying to mentally count the times, but after a while he draws a blank. "I dunno man. Maybe thirty? Forty?"

Fuck.

Forty times my boyfriend was cheating on me with my friends, and I was oblivious. It crosses my mind that I should be angry right now. Furious, even. But the only thing I feel is disappointment that I've missed forty chances to watch this happen.

"Forty times we've hooked up," Paul corrects him. "But a bunch of those times we went more than one round at a time."

I see Kenneth's eyes look up at me, and he gives me a wink.

"How does that make you feel, cuck?" Paul asks.

"Sorry I missed it."

The room erupts in laughter.

"O damn, I'm sorry, man." I can't tell if Paul's actually apologetic, or if he's just trolling me. "Hey, how about we get this on video? Then you can jack off to it any time you like." He looks around. "Someone get some video of this!"

A couple of people get out phones and start filming. James gets in close for a good shot of Kenneth's mouth, stuffed full of Adam's cock. I know he's not doing it just for my benefit; I know what that asshole's go-to porn vid is going to be from now on.

"Maybe we'll edit this all together and make you a video," Adam suggests. "Then whenever Kenneth's being fucked by one of us when you're not around, at least you'll have that to jack off to."

The way they're making jokes at my expense gets me even harder. I can feel my dick throb, and I need to grab it so bad. But I'm grateful I can't, because I feel like I'd cum in a second right now, and I know I've still got a long show ahead of me.

Paul picks up the pace, pumping Kenneth's ass hard and fast now. Every time he pulls his cock out almost to the tip, I get a good look at its full length just for an instant, before it plunges back in. It's so slick, so fat. So superior. Kenneth's muffled moans are getting more ragged, and Paul's grunting each time he slams his cock in hard. I can tell he's about to cum. He's so close, he's dead focused on Kenneth's ass. But then for a second he looks at me, and grins. "I'm about to breed your boy."

My dick spasms at that, and I can feel it oozing precum. I can't help but let out a little gasp. "Fuck!"

Paul's looking me right in the eyes, laughing at me, as he lets his load loose inside Kenneth. While the other guys cheer, he just keeps looking right at me, his chest heaving, while he catches his breath. He slowly pulls his cock out, and as he does a trickle of semen runs out of Kenneth's ass and down his leg. He gets up and walks over to me. Right up to me, so his slowly deflating cock, covered with the slick shine of his own cum, is right in front of my face. He looks down at me, and asks me, "Enjoy that, cuck?"

I don't answer. I don't know how to answer. It doesn't matter though, I can tell he already knows how I feel. He can tell how much it's turning me on to be made a laughing stock in front of all my friends, and to lose my boyfriend to each of them one by one. And he can tell I'm being torn up inside by the shame of coming to terms with how much I love it.

Paul gives me a pat on the shoulder and wanders off to get some beer. Adam's head is buried in Kenneth's ass, licking the cum out, while James has replaced him in Kenneth's mouth. James is grinning at me, enjoying my humiliation as much as he seems to be enjoying the blowjob. He's got his phone out, and he's filming Kenneth sucking on his cock. At one stage he points the phone at me, and asks, "You enjoying it, dude?"

I just nod.

"What was that? Couldn't hear you," he kept pushing. "I was asking if you're enjoying seeing your boyfriend sucking on my cock."

He's such an asshole. He's loving it. Of course he's loving it - he's always so fucking smug when he jokes about wanting to fuck Kenneth. Only now I realise that all this time when I thought it was just his fantasy, he'd probably been fucking him all along.

Adam's done rimming Kenneth's hole and he's fucking him now, making out with Paul as he does. They've settled into a rhythm, like they've done this a hundred times. James is filming Kenneth again, talking dirty to him, egging Adam on to fuck him harder. A few my friends are egging them on, slowly stroking their own dicks, while others have settled into just chatting and drinking beers while they watch the show taking place on the living room floor.

I have no idea how quickly time's passing. I'm still transfixed on the sight. Kenneth is coated in a sweaty sheen, blissfully backing up on Adam's cock over, and over again. Once Adam finally cums inside him, and slowly withdraws his cum-slicked cock, James is ready to take over.

"Hey cuckold, you gonna beg me?" he asks. He's so obnoxious, but tonight for the first time that just seems to make him hot. I think I'd always felt a little superior to him, knowing how desperate he was to fuck my man. But now, knowing that he'll actually get to — and knowing that the smug grins he's always giving me were probably actually because he'd been fucking Kenneth behind my back the whole time — now I feel completely inferior to him.

"Fuck, James." I can feel the warmth in my face; the embarrassment, the anger, the resentment, the lust. "Fuck him, please. I want to see you fuck him."

James laughs at me, and slams his cock into Kenneth's ass in one smooth motion. Kenneth cries out, cradling his head on his arms on the carpet, as James starts to jackhammer his ass. He slaps his ass hard, grabs his hair and pulls his head closer so his back is forced to arch. The more Kenneth wails, the harder James fucks him. It's only a couple of minutes before beads of sweat are starting to roll down his forehead. He looks focused, his jaw clenched as he fucks him as hard as he can. I can tell he's getting close, faster and harder.

"You want me to cum in your ass?" he asks.

"Of course!" Kenneth moans in response.

"Fucking beg, slut," he demands.

Kenneth is crying out "Breed me! Fuck! Breed me!"

With a roar, James collapses on top of Kenneth and unloads deep inside him. Kenneth sinks to the ground, and James lies there on top of him, chest heaving as he catches his breath.

"Does your cuck boyfriend ever fuck you like that?" he asks, breathlessly.

"No. Never."

I can feel my dick leaking.

As they lie there recovering, someone asks who's up next. There's a moment of silence before Ewan volunteers himself.

"Fuck." I don't know if I can handle this one.

He pulls off his shirt. I've never paid that much attention to it before, but he's in pretty good shape. Broad chest and shoulders, textbook dad bod. He pulls his pants and underwear off in one go, and in an instant I see how much bigger his dick is than mine.

James gets up off Kenneth, and Kenneth gets up off the floor. He and Ewan start to kiss, and Kenneth plays with Ewan's balls until his cock starts to swell.

As they're doing that, James comes up to me, his cock in front of my face. "You gonna clean me off?" he asks.

For a second I'm kind of disturbed by the thought; I've never felt any kind of sexual attraction to James.

"There's four guys' cum on here," he says, shaking his softening cock in front of me. "All of them from inside your boy's ass."

Without a word I try to reach his cock with my mouth. But the shackles are holding me in place too tight to reach.

He looks down at me, laughs at me, and brings his junk closer. He slowly puts his cock into my mouth, and wrap my lips around it. I can taste the salty cum immediately. I run my tongue all over it, tasting every millimetre, getting as much as I possibly can of the cum that he's drawn from my boyfriend's ass. James grabs me by the jaw and tilts my head so I'm looking up at his face while I lick the cum off him. That smug, shit-eating grin on his face, relishing how much he's degrading me.

Eventually he pulls out his dick without a word. I want to lunge for it, to get any last bit of greasy cum that I can. But I restrain myself; besides, I'm distracted by the sight of Ewan fucking Kenneth on the sofa. I can barely get my head around it; all these years of friendship, going back to when we were young, me thinking Ewan was 'my straight friend'. The times I'd crushed on him over the course of our friendship, fanta- sised about the what-ifs, and told myself to get over it because he was only interested in women. And all this time, all he needed was the right piece of ass. My boyfriend's ass. And he was so willing to fuck me over like this. I don't know how I'll ever be able to look at Ewan again after this.

It's like he reads my mind: "Our hangouts are never gonna be quite the same after this, eh bro?"

There's a few chuckles from around the room.

"For you, at least," he corrects himself. "We've been doing this for ages, so it's nothing out of the ordinary for us."

I think about how many times the two of them must have snuck out and fucked while I was oblivious, or met up in secret. I can't help but let a tear escape my eye, and another few drops of cum leak out of my erect penis.

Ewan's close. It's a small mercy that at least he hasn't lasted that long. I can see his jaw tense, like he's trying to solve a complicated problem. He pounds Kenneth harder, jerking his dick as he fucks him. He looks at me. "You ready to see me give your boyfriend a bit of my DNA?"

He doesn't wait for my response; he just lets loose inside Kenneth with a "fuuuuucck!"

Josh is already naked and waiting for his turn when Ewan pulls out. Kenneth looks up at him and begs him, "Fuck me."

But Josh has something else in mind. "Get up, slut," he says, grinning. As Kenneth pulls himself up off the sofa, Josh leads him over towards me. "Let's give your boyfriend a bit of a show."

Kenneth smiles. He's into it. He bends over and puts his hands on my knees. His face his only a couple of centimetres away from mine; I can see the colour of his flushed cheeks, and every bead of sweat on his forehead. He looks like he's leaning in to kiss me. But he doesn't kiss me. Instead he lets out a whimper as Josh enters him from behind. I look up at Josh's face, towering over me as he holds Kenneth by the hips and thrusts into him.

With each thrust, Kenneth's head is pushed closer to mine. He closes his eyes tight, pushing through the pain and concentrating on the pleasure. They're closed so tight that the skin on his forehead and around his eyes is crumpled up. I can feel the warmth of his ragged breathing as he lets out little moans in time with Josh's thrusts.

Even though Kenneth looks like he can barely handle the intensity of this fuck, Josh looks so casual as he pumps away that he could be waiting for a bus or something. He asks me in a conversational tone, "Hey so Cole, did you suspect I was fucking your boyfriend?"

I shake my head. I'm wracking my brains, but seriously, I never even had an inkling. Fuck, I'm an idiot.

"I've been coming over twice a week for months," he mocks me. "Best way to start my morning."

Kenneth breathlessly confesses, "Sometimes he fucks me in our bed."

Josh laughs. "You know, every time we fuck in your bed I wipe my cock clean on your pillow. You've been sleeping with your face in my dried up cum for months."

I moan involuntarily at that. I feel my dick pulse, hard. And again. No, fuck, not yet. But it's too late. The look on Kenneth's face, the sounds of his moans, the taunting of my next-door neighbour, the vivid image of them making love in my bed, the fantasy of burying my head in Josh's dried up cum on my pillow, it's all way, way too much. My dick pulses, and jerks, and I feel the orgasm rise up out of me. My dick convulses as a flow of thick cum starts to erupt out of it's head.

The crowd sees. They whoop and cheer for my unwanted ejaculation. There are high-fives, and laughs, and jokes at my expense. Kenneth opens is eyes, looks down at the cum soaking into my jeans, and chuckles. He gives me a peck on the lips. "One down."

Now Josh has got the outcome he wants, he takes Kenneth back to the sofa. He lies him down on his back, legs up in the air. Staying standing, he lifts Kenneth's hips up off the sofa, and Kenneth instinctively wraps his legs around his body as he enters him again. As I feel my dick soften and shrivel, I watch them fuck like that on the sofa.

As the novelty of my cuckolding has started to wear off, the gang in the living room is focusing less on the action. Instead they're settling into an easy, relaxed rhythm, casually chatting among themselves with one eye on the live sex show. I'm watching intently though, and I can tell from Kenneth's ragged breathing that Josh is close to making him cum. He confirms it when he whispers, "Fuck, I'm gonna cum man." Josh keeps his steady rhythm, thrusting deep into Kenneth's ass while he kisses his neck and his jaw line. Kenneth starts to wail. "Fuck!" It gets the crowd's attention; they know what's about to happen. "Fuck!" I see his body tense, then convulse, over and over again as the semen seeps through the fabric of his jockstrap. Josh keeps fucking him for another few seconds before his body, too, tenses up as he releases his load inside Kenneth.

Panting and chuckling together, they collapse in a pile on the sofa and make out for a while. Then Josh gets up off him, and goes to grab a couple of beers, not even bothering to put his underwear on. His heavy, thick cock swings around as he strolls back across the room to hand Kenneth a beer.

Kenneth reclines on the sofa and starts to neck down his beer.

"That's not it, is it?" Shaun asks. "I haven't had a go yet!"

"Course not! I'm just taking a break," Kenneth reassures him. "How 'bout you go next after I've caught my breath?"

"You're on."

Adam asks me if I want a drink. I accept; I need it after that experience. He unlocks one of my shackles; "I'd better not see you touch that dick, or else this is going back on," he tells me sternly as he hands me a beer.

Kenneth is still centre of attention. While he throws back a beer over the other side of the room, my friends' hands are all over his ass. He excuses himself for a second and comes over to me.

"Hey babe. You enjoying yourself?"

"I can't believe you did this." I try to sound mad, but Kenneth interprets it completely the opposite way. I'm not sure if that's genuine or if he's just playing with me.

"I knew you'd love it," he tells me. "How hot was it to be outed as a cuck in front of your friends?"

I feel the warmth of blood rushing to my cheeks in embarrassment, followed by the feeling of blood rushing to my dick when I think about the shame of being emasculated like that in front of all of them.

"You ready for some more, babe?"

I should be desperate for this to be over. Shouldn't I? But I want to see more. I want to see every last man in the room take my boyfriend from me and use him. I want to see every one of their faces as they cum inside him, and his face as he takes each new cock. I want to see all the ways other men can make him feel, that I'll never be able to.

I nod. "Yeah." I'm sure of this. I look around the room and call out, "Who's next?"

Charlie volunteers. He bends Kenneth over, facing away from me, so that all I can see are the muscles tensing in Charlie's ass and back as he pumps away. After a while he props one leg up on the sofa itself, so I can get a decent view of his ballsack slapping against Kenneth's ass while he fucks him.

Once Charlie's given him a decent working over, Luca and Shaun tag in. Kenneth lies down on his back of the floor and his legs braced against Luca's shoulders while Luca slides his decently thick cock into his sloppy hole. Kenneth tilts his head right back so Shaun can get his cock straight down his throat. James pulls out his phone again and films the two of them spitroasting him, Kenneth gagging and gasping for air the whole time.

After Luca's done, Shaun removes his cock from

Kenneth's throat and moves round to his ass. But he's already close, and it's only a couple of minutes before he's blowing his load. Then it's Brett's turn; he flips Kenneth over face down, pins him down and fucks him from behind on the floor. As he gets faster, and closer to his climax, he pulls Kenneth up into a kind of almost-doggy, and pounds him hard till he nuts in his ass too.

Finally, there's only one person left who hasn't had a go. Kenneth walks over to Joseph. "Saved the best till last," he says, grinning at him.

Joseph's jeans are already undone, and it's easy to make out the shape of his fat, hard cock in his underwear. Kenneth lowers himself down onto Joseph's crotch and writhes on it, getting it ready to fuck. The way he whimpers is like nothing I've ever heard before; it's like an expression of pure, urgent desperation. He begs Joseph, "Fuck me, fuck me please."

Joseph flips his cock out of his underwear, but I can't see it because it's obscured by Kenneth in his lap. Kenneth keeps rubbing up and down on him, getting himself more and more worked up at the thought of being fucked.

Finally Joseph takes his cock and lines it up against Kenneth's hole. For the first time I can see it properly. And fuck, it's a monster. If you'd asked me before tonight, I would have said that Kenneth probably couldn't take a cock that size. But as I see the tip of Joseph's cock penetrate Kenneth's hole, and then slowly slide further and further inside, stretching him wider than I thought could possibly be plea-surable, there's no mistaking Kenneth's moan of pure pleasure.

Joseph stops mid way in. Then he looks me right in the eyes, gives me an arrogant asshole smirk, and then plunges his cock into Kenneth balls deep in one movement. Kenneth lets out a pained gasp, and for a second I think it must be too much for him. But then I can tell by the way slowly lets out the word "fuck!", and leans his head back, that he's in heaven right now.

The two of them kiss, passionately. Kenneth starts to ride Joseph. It's slow and sexy and lustful, and Kenneth is a mess of muffled moans and gasps as he takes all of the man's cock inside him.

An awkward silence descends on the room, as everyone seems to realise how completely lost in each other Kenneth and Joseph are. Suddenly it feels like we're all intruding on an intimate moment, and that neither of them even realise we're there. I suddenly feel sick to my stomach seeing my boyfriend not just get fucked, but make love, with a level of intimacy and intensity I never expected. My cock is throbbing so hard watching them make love, but I resist the urge to touch it because I know I'll blow my load again in a second if I do.

Everyone else seems almost as blown away by the spectacle as I am. Kenneth has ripped Joseph's shirt off him, revealing a thick, muscular chest with a cover of dark hair. He's sucking and biting on his nipples, and Joseph is growling with appreciation. Joseph has freed Kenneth's cock from the pouch of his jockstrap, and is jacking it in long, slow strokes. Kenneth is riding him harder and harder by the second. Each time, I see Joseph's slick, cum-covered cock pushing in and out of him.

Kenneth's breathing is ragged. He keeps gasping, "Oh my god. Oh my god."

Joseph is kissing his collarbone, his neck, his ear, his jawline. His arms rest lazily on Kenneth's hips as Kenneth bounces up and down on top of him. He looks up for a second, looks over at me, sees the expression on my face, and laughs. He whispers in Kenneth's ear, and Kenneth laughs too.

They fuck harder, faster, more urgently. Kenneth buries his chest in Joseph's shoulder as his gasps and his whimpers become uncontrollable. "Fuck! Fuck! O shit! Fuck!" He must be so close now. "Kiss me!"

Joseph takes Kenneth's head in both hands, brings it up to his face, and kisses him. Kenneth lifts up, so that only the tip of Joseph's cock is still inside. Then with one, last, slow movement he slides back down onto Joseph's cock one more time. He lets out a howl, and although I can't see the ropes of cum shoot from his dick I know that he's just ejaculated. His face collapses back into Joseph's shoulder.

The room is stunned silent, except for the sounds of Kenneth's breath heaving. It's not often you see a fuck like that, and everyone knows it.

It's almost a full minute before Kenneth regains his composure enough to say, "Fuck, man. That was incredible."

Joseph smirks again. He kisses Kenneth on the neck. "I'm not done yet," he tells him softly, but loud enough for the room to hear.

"Really?"

"I'm close," Joseph says. "And I want the last load inside you tonight to be mine. You want that?"

"Yes."

"Tell the cuck."

Kenneth turns around, as though he's only just remembering I'm even there. "I want him to cum inside me, babe. Do you want him to—"

"Do it." I don't need him to finish the question. My dick throbs so hard when I say those words, and for a second I lose all my self control and grab it. But just the slightest touch is enough to set me off again. I pull my hand away but it's already too late; my dick throbs, and again, and then I'm releasing my second load in a slow trickle.

Joseph laughs. He starts to pump Kenneth's ass, hard. Kenneth wails and gasps, as Joseph's huge dick destroys him. "Please cum in me soon," Kenneth begs, "I don't know how much of this I can take!"

Joseph obliges. He lets out a grunt, and at that moment he slows completely to a stop. I can see his cock pulse as it releases its seed inside Kenneth's body.

The two of them just sit there for a minute or so, Joseph's cock still inside Kenneth, Kenneth's head still resting on Joseph's shoulders. The others at the party, suddenly seeming to realise the awkwardness of watching them in this moment, start to dissipate to get drinks or talk to each other.

Finally Kenneth gets up off Joseph. A glob of semen drips out of him as he gets up, and I can now see the cum Kenneth left behind all over Joseph's chest.

I count through it in my head: the tally's at eleven. My boyfriend has just taken eleven loads in his ass, and made me watch every one of them. There's eleven guys' cum all over his ass; it's trickling out of him, down his legs. It's all over the sofa, and there's a pool of it on the floor.

Everyone in the room turns and looks at me expectantly. But I have no idea what to say.

Paul breaks the silence though. "Looks like Cole got cucked hard tonight, huh boys?" And with that, everyone in the room is laughing at my humiliation again.

As Paul and Adam unlock me from my restraints, Kenneth gets the music going and gets a few of the guys dancing. Two or three grind up against him, him still naked apart from his jockstrap thats soaked in cum and sweat and lube. I don't even notice when the restraints are off, I just sit there, watching Kenneth's naked ass and back pressing up against Joseph's body as they move to the music.

A couple of the guys try to make conversation, but I'm too mesmerised by the sight, and too shellshocked by the whole experience, to even string together a few sentences.

After half an hour or so the party winds down. Kenneth's still dancing, his partners changing every few minutes as more of my friends take a turn with him. But one by one, they start saying their goodbyes and heading out the door. They all thank me for a great night, none of them able to keep a straight face. "Best birthday ever," Ewan tells me with a grin as he heads out the door. "I hope you realise I'm gonna fuck your boyfriend every birthday from now on!"

Eventually just about everyone has gone. There's only me, Kenneth and Joseph left. Kenneth comes over, sits down in my lap, and kisses me.

"Happy birthday baby," he whispers. "Did you like it?"

I honestly have no idea what to say. This has been the most shameful, sickening night of my life. I've been betrayed, and degraded, by everyone I thought cared about me. And all orchestrated by the man who I thought loved me the most.

But at the same time, it's been the most intensely arousing thing that has ever happened to me. And the humiliation has made it even hotter.

All I can say is "I love you."

"I love you too," Kenneth replies, and kisses me again.

"I am shattered though," I admit. "I just want to go to sleep." I look over and notice that Joseph is still here though, casually flicking through something on his phone. I tilt my head in his direction. "Hey do you think you can get him to go so we can go to bed?"

"Oh, Joseph's staying here tonight."

"Kenneth, what the fuck?"

Joseph looks up, obviously having heard us talking about him. "Since it's your birthday you can sleep in the bedroom though," he tells me nonchalantly. "There's room on the floor."

CHAPTER 12
KENNETH

I wake up and the sun is streaming through the bedroom window. My mouth's dry and my head's sore, nothing too serious though. Lucky I stopped drinking pretty early last night. My ass though, that's another story. Man, it feels like I've had a steam train role through there. As I stretch in the bed I can feel the stickiness of cum on my ass and my thighs; there must have been so much in there that it would have been leaking out all night. I think back and I remember how, after all that, Joseph had fucked me again just as I was starting to go to sleep.

I roll over, and nestle my face against Joseph's muscular shoulder. I lay my arm on his chest, and gently rub the bristly hair on it.

I see him start to stir. His mouth moves, and he shakes his head slowly from side to side. He lets out a sigh that's more like a growl, as he slowly opens his eyes. It takes a few seconds for him to wake and focus, and when he does, he looks down at me.

"Morning," I whisper.

"Morning." He rests a hand on my shoulder, and closes his eyes again.

Even though I'm tired, hungover, and physically exhausted from the fucking I was given last night, I'm still wide awake now. I realise that I'm desperate for Joseph to wake up. I try to resist the urge to paw at him and disturb him.

A minute later he opens his eyes again. It feels firm and gentle at the same time when he runs his hand down my arm. He looks at me, then kisses me. The bristles of his beard feel soft on my face.

"My mouth is so dry," he tells me. He looks down to where Cole is lying on the floor. I can't see Cole's sleeping position from where I am in the bed, but he sits up immediately and I can see a look that's eager and fearful and ashamed, in equal parts.

"Get us some water," Joseph orders. The disappointment is written all over Cole's face; I don't know what he was expecting to happen, that we'd all sit around having a chat about the previous night's events? He casts his eyes down, gets up off the floor, and goes to get water.

A minute later he comes back with two glasses of water. He sets one down on the bedside table for me, and he hesitantly hands the other one to Joseph. Joseph gulps his down in a few mouthfuls.

"Morning hun," Cole says to me. "How are you feeling?"

Before I can answer, Joseph interjects. "Out."

Cole looks at me, silently pleading. A real man would tell Joseph to fuck off and get out of his bed. But no way Cole was going to do that. I just look at him and do the "sorry" shrug of the shoulders. Cole slowly walks out of the room.

"Shut the door behind you."

The door shuts.

Joseph kisses me again, roughly. He pins me down, his body on top of mine. My legs instinctively go up in the air, either side of him. He kisses my neck, then my collarbone and my nipple, then he kisses my mouth again. Effortlessly he slides his cock into me; it's still lubed from last night. It hurts like hell, but nothing in the world feels more perfect than his cock in me. I gasp.

He pulls it all the way out, and slams it back in. The head-board bangs against the wall. I can't help whimpering. Feeling him slide in and out of me, his weight fully on me, his torso heaving against mine as he fucks me, it's like something I can't even describe. It's like I'm half of a broken object and he's the other half, and the cum leaking out of me is the glue that's going to put us back together.

He fucks me savagely. Then he stops for a second, and looks me dead in the eyes. "You know you're mine now."

I nod. "I'm yours." I mean it.

"Good."

"Don't stop fucking me, please."

CHAPTER 13
COLE

Kenneth's on his feet as soon as he hears the sound of the door opening. He runs to the front door to greet Joseph. Although I can't see from where I'm sitting, I've seen it enough times now to know exactly what's happening. He's wrapped in Joseph's thick arms, and he's got his arms wrapped around Joseph's neck. They're kissing and whispering to each other. I can picture the look of adoration in Kenneth's eyes.

Then they're off up the stairs, and Joseph calls out in his booming, authoritative voice: "Dinner in an hour."

I give it a minute, then I quietly creep upstairs and sit outside the bedroom door. I can hear the muttering of them talking, then the sound of the bed creaking as they get to it. Most of the words I can't make out, but I definitely hear when Kenneth says, "I love you." A few seconds after that and all I can hear is the sound of the bedsprings creaking and the headboard slamming against the wall, along with the sound of Kenneth moaning. It didn't take them long to get into it. It never does, especially when they've had to wait over a week to see each other.

I listen for a few minutes, but then I figure I'd better go get dinner started. They'll be hungry once they're done.

I take my time cooking because I know they'll take their time fucking. I can hear them through the ceiling. I'm pretty used to this now: cooking dinner with my cock rock hard in my pants, listening to Kenneth and Joseph making love above me.

It's good timing; the vegetables roasting in the oven look just about done when I hear the bedroom door open and someone head to the bathroom, and the rest of the food is just coming together too. By the time I'm dishing everything up the two of them are coming down the stairs, both unclothed except for their underwear. Kenneth's ass looks just as good as ever. But to be honest, when the two of them hang around the house semi-naked like this, the thing I really can't stop staring at is the big bulge of Joseph's cock and balls in his briefs. I think about how his cock is probably still slick from being inside Kenneth. For a second it makes me a little sad, but it also makes my penis throb a little too.

I hand them dinner. Kenneth thanks me enthusiastically. "Thanks, babe, this looks great!"

Joseph takes the bowl from me like it's his god-given right, without acknowledging me at all.

We eat in front of the TV. The two of them wolf their food down. I wonder if they're in a hurry to get back to it. But somewhat surprisingly, after they've finished eating, they settle into the sofa together, Kenneth resting against Joseph's chest.

We watch TV for while. I'm on the other sofa, pretending to watch the tv too, although in reality I don't even notice what's on because my entire mind is consumed with desperately trying not to watch them together.

"Hey we're going to go meet up with Paul and Adam tomorrow night," Kenneth tells me.

"Oh cool," I say. To be honest things haven't been the

same with them since my party, and the idea of seeing them makes me a little nervous. But I can't let this ruin my friendships, and besides, that's not something I want to admit to Kenneth. And it only takes a second or two before my dick hardens a little again, wondering if they might end up with their cocks inside my boyfriend again. "What time do I need to be there? I have a work thing but it should be over by about seven."

"Um, I meant Joseph and me."

It feels like being kicked in the balls. "Seriously? They're my friends."

Kenneth looks at me with a hint of annoyance. "They're my friends too. And they wanted to get to know Joseph. "

I look over at Joseph, who says nothing, but has that arrogant smirk on his face that he always has.

"Look, I guess you can come if you want." It sounds more like a question than a statement, and he looks at Joseph as he says it, who looks back dispassionately. "We're going out for a drink, then we're probably going back to their place to fuck. Or we might come here, who knows. You can watch if you want."

For fuck's sake, that's insulting. I picture them, all out together like old friends. And then I picture them all falling asleep together, spent from fucking. It gets me a little bit harder.

"I'll let you know," I tell him. I know that I'll probably just stay home because none of them want me to be there. But the thought of missing out on seeing them fuck drives me wild.

"Maybe you guys should come back here after," I add, after a pause.

I get up. "Anyway, I'm going to bed." As I walk past, I fight off the urge to give Kenneth a kiss goodnight. I know that's not how it works when Joseph's here. Instead I keep walking.

"G'night Cole," Kenneth calls out behind me.

I brush my teeth, and get into bed in the spare room. Five minutes or so later, I hear the door to the master bedroom shut. I close my eyes and picture what they're doing in there. Another few minutes later and I hear the bed start to creak, and the familiar pounding on the wall. I hear Kenneth moan, and I hear him scream "Fuck me! Fuck me!"

I take out my cock, and I start to jerk off. I hope it doesn't last too long; I want to hear Joseph cum before I do. But it never happens that way, he can go for hours. When I hear Joseph growling "yeah, you love that cock" and I hear Kenneth moan "yes, I love you, I love your cock!" I can't take it any longer and I blow a load all over myself.

If I'm lucky, I'll have time to get hard again before they're finished.